CHI

BENTLEY

AND THE GHOST
OF ASHER WORTH

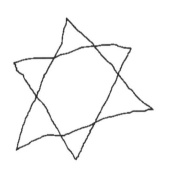

M.J. COLEWOOD

For:

My Father, Brian

Also in the *Chester Bentley Mysteries:*

Book '0':

THE WARTIME THIEF
- A NOVELLA -

*(Go to www.mjcolewood.com now
and download the exciting novella for free)*

Book II:

THE LAST TREASURE
OF ANCIENT ENGLAND

Book III:

THE KING OF PIRATES

Acknowledgements

Thanks to Kirsty for her timely comments, once again, as well as María Augustí, Sam Ber, Sam Coke & Vittorio Scaliani

SIC PARVIS MAGNA
'Thus great things from small things (come)'

PROLOGUE

The greatest mysteries often begin at home - one only has to look more closely to find them. In the case of Chester Bentley, his first great mystery, like most great mysteries, started with a scream...

THE SCREAM
Plymouth, 1981

Lucy Hartley had always prided herself on being a rational woman, but now she stood gripped by cold fear at the bottom of the staircase. She had been in the house just a year and nothing out of the ordinary had happened, but for some uncanny reason, she instinctively felt as if that time had come to an end and now, in that precise instant, she would confront her worst fears. She looked up at the domed Victorian skylight and breathed in deeply. Then with heavy feet, she began her courageous ascent.

She struggled to master her nerves as she spoke to herself: *Keep it together, Lucy. There can't be any truth to this, no matter what the cleaning lady said. But then why did you tell the children she had left because she was allergic to the cat and not just come out with the truth? Because it was too horrible to utter such words! Keep calm. Keep walking. Nothing will happen. Have some faith. When you get to the upper landing simply enter the bedroom, drop your things and leave. The cleaning lady was just making things up. But what are you saying, Lucy? Stop deceiving yourself!*

Lucy reached the top of the stairs. Her legs felt light now and as her hand left the ornate banister, she suddenly felt giddy. She forced herself to look at the menacing bedroom door. It seemed to beckon her to open it, as if it were charged with energy, as if someone else was in the house. And yet, she was the only living being present in the enormous residence.

Don't go in! Don't do it! Lucy screamed inside, but she had to. She didn't know why, but she just *had to*. She twisted the brass doorknob, pushed the heavy door back on its creaking hinges and, anaesthetized by fear, stepped into the room. She had a moment's relief before all was lost as terror coursed through her body like a violent volcanic eruption. She saw it. It was real. She screamed as if death had possessed her, a primaeval sound she had never thought herself capable of making. Then the thing moved, and she turned to run. As she did so, she distinctly felt something brush through her hair, trying to grab at her. In her adrenalin induced panic, she leapt down the entire first flight of stairs, flying with superhuman strength as if her very survival depended upon her immediate escape, whatever the cost. She landed with her hand following the banister and flung herself down the second flight of stairs. She didn't dare look behind her, she couldn't look behind her. She collapsed in a heap at the bottom of the stairs, miraculously intact. Then, with one final effort, she sprang to her feet, breathing like a wild animal and rushed forward just as her husband was opening the front door on his return from work. She flew past him, screaming, into the afternoon sunshine.

Two weeks later, the house was sold; Lucy Hartley and her family began life elsewhere.

Despite the fresh start though, Mrs Hartley would never be the same again. The moment she had opened that bedroom door she had witnessed something that everyone has talked about, but few have ever experienced. That sight and her screams would echo through her dreams forever more.

PART ONE
- GHOST -

THE WATCH
Lizard Point, Cornish Coast 1588

The two men stoked the fire in their stone beehive hut, the welcome warmth fending off the morning chill that blew against the Cornish coast. From their lookout on The Lizard, they were perched on the edge of the world, with nothing but the Atlantic Ocean before them. The watchmen occasionally looked up from the flames to scan the horizon, and then returned to their toasted bread, breathing a sigh of relief that the sea was still empty of any signs of human life.

"July 19th," said John, in his West Country tone, "it's me Saint's Day tomorrow, St. John Plessington."

"Let's hope you live to see it then," joked Mark.

"You think they'll be landed here in Cornwall?"

"Too far from London, they'll come ashore further up all right."

"But you'd like it if they put ashore right here in Cornwall, wouldn't you?"

"What you be meaning by that then!"

"You're a Catholic."

"I'll have you know that the first contingent of troops for the defence of England against the King of Spain was raised by Viscount Montague, a Catholic nobleman."

John returned to staring into the flames, wishing he hadn't put his friend to the test.

"Don't let the threat of invasion play tricks with your mind," continued John, "we pray to the same God, just in different ways. It is his decision, and his alone, as to which one of us errs in our ways. That is, of course, if such trivial things matter to one so great, which I believe they do not."

"Is it not blasphemous to utter such talk?"

"I'm talking of the beliefs of men, not the acts of God, thou pox-marked miscreant."

"But…" John suddenly stopped speaking. His bread fell into the fire and began to burn. Mark looked to see John's face fixed on the horizon, uninterested in his smouldering crust. It was then that he too felt the forceful suspicion that an enemy was in their midst.

John stepped out of the tight confines of the hut and lifted his hand, pointing out into the distance, "It's… it's the…" Both men's hearts began to pound, and their breathing grew rapid as they spotted the very sails they had dreaded.

"Light the beacon!" commanded Mark, turning to grab the torch from inside the hut. He plunged it into the fire, rushing back out with the bulbous head of the staff now ablaze. John followed suit and they both marched up to the highest point just behind the hut where a large signal beacon stood waiting to be ignited. Mark turned to wait for John. Together they mounted the stone-based structure and then drove their torches into the brushwood which was held up high in a metal-framed basket. The hopeful fire crackled, spat and popped until a strong wind caught the flame and it roared ferociously into life.

John dropped his torch and left it to burn where it lay. He stepped forward and looked up the coast, smiling as another fire burst into life and shortly after that another, and then another pinhead of light erupted in the distance as the fires leapt along the arch of the dark coastline.

"In an hour London will know," said John.

"And York in 12."

"The Armada is upon us."

"Every man must put himself in and be ready."

"May the Lord have mercy on our souls."

They turned to see that a great part of the horizon had now disappeared and in its place was a mass of vessels and sail, the like of which they had never seen before, and it had England in its sights.

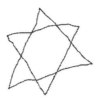

CHESTER BENTLEY
Plymouth, 1981

Chester Bentley lay fast asleep, dreaming of his favourite vanilla ice-cream, when suddenly it started to lick him back and wouldn't stop. He raised his hands to fight it off. Then he noticed the faint whiff of rotten fish, which soon became unbearable as it lathered his entire face.

"Chester?"

Someone called his name.

"Chester!"

He sat bolt upright. His eyes focused on Sherlock, his Jack Russell, who was licking his face keenly, waking him up.

"Oh no!" he thought. "I've overslept."

"Come on, Chester! We're going to be late… again!" now he recognised the voice, it was his mother, calling impatiently.

Bentley grumbled, stirred and stumbled out of bed toward his armchair where his crumpled clothes lay from the day before. He tried to make up for lost time and do three things at once. As he buttoned his shirt with one hand, he fastened his belt with another while forcing a foot into a shoe. He then flew down the staircase and out of the door, completely bypassing his parents in the hall as he whooshed past them. He combed his hand through his dark hair in a weak attempt to brush it, noting with resignation the ever-present antenna of hair that stuck up at the back. He tried to flatten it, but it bounced back up in protest.

Bentley pulled at the car door only to find that it was locked. He looked inside - it was empty. What on earth?! he thought, and then turned round, back towards the house. His father stood there in the entrance, his hands behind his back. His mother had hers folded in front of her.

"Isn't it school today?" he asked, suspecting what his parents were about to say.

"If it were," said his mother, "you'd at least be wearing your uniform!"

Bentley glanced down at the jeans and t-shirt under his school blazer. "So, why—"

"Prep-school is not for another week," explained his father despairingly. "We're *moving house* today. Come on, you're eleven now, it's high time you started to take responsibility and remembered things, son, instead of expecting us to tell you what you have to do all the time."

Bentley walked back into the bare building and began moving his stuff downstairs. It was then that he remembered why they had decided to move house in the first place and wasn't sure if the house they were moving into was any better.

- III -

BETTER THE DEVIL YOU KNOW
Plymouth, 1981

A brief drive later and the car was turning in through a set of modest black gates and up the long, private drive of a grand row of mid-Victorian semi-detached houses. Bentley peered out at his new home. To the right was a communal, yet private walled garden for the fortunate residents to stroll in. Then he noticed someone behind the bushes staring at him and up at the house as the car pulled up.

The moment the man realised Bentley had spotted him, he darted out of sight. It made an uneasy impression on Bentley. Why was someone so interested in his house? he wondered, and then the thought was gone.

The car parked up and Bentley walked in through the heavy white doors that opened into a black and white tiled entrance. A set of delicate internal doors then led into the elegant hallway.

"You remember where your room is, do you?" asked his father.

"Yes, out the back, up the spiral staircase."

"Right you are. You can start by taking up all your things and then come back to help us with the rest of the house."

Bentley poked his head into the front room, which was made up of two rooms connected by a large archway with a fireplace at either end. His mother was already sizing it up for her chandeliers. Mother's little obsession, he thought. How he feared standing under her chandeliers. He turned back to the hall and looked up at the delicate lead-framed skylight that let light pour in from the heavens.

The box in his hands was beginning to feel heavy, so he hurried on through the dining-room, glancing at the neat garden outside the French windows as he went. The kitchen led into the boot room and the rear entrance. Bentley crossed the flagstones and left the elegant house behind him, and instead entered a rustic cottage with dark slate walls.

At the end of the room, and sprouting out of the stone floor, was an ornate metal staircase that spiralled vertically like a corkscrew. Its coiled structure rattled gently as he followed it up through the ceiling. When he reached the small landing, he turned left into his bedroom, which felt miles away from his parents' room.

Now that he was there on his own, he noticed the silence and solitude for the first time and, for some inexplicable reason, it felt eerie. It was not the first time he had felt that way and he instinctively knew something was awry. If he screamed out in the night, no one would hear him. He was cut off.

They had moved to get away from such strange goings on in their last house, his mother had felt it too and insisted they move. But now they were here, Bentley wasn't so sure they had made the right decision. They may well have been better off where they were. They at least went about their day without any interference, but here, in this large old house, Bentley believed they would not be left in peace. Sometimes it was certainly better the devil you know, or in the case of Bentley it was better the spirit he had met.

For a second, he felt a tinge of fear creeping up on him and wished he had chosen a room closer to the front of the house, nearer his parents. However, he had been the one insisting on having the room with its own private washroom. Now though, he stared unimpressed at the sunken bath, seeming more like a sarcophagus. "Who lived here before? Cleopatra?" he mumbled. Yet there could be no admitting he was wrong in front of his parents. He would lose face. After all, he would be a teenager soon.

He put the box down and quickly returned to get more of his belongings, telling himself to stop being a baby.

CANDLES IN THE WIND
Plymouth, 1981

"Big day tomorrow," said his mother as she carefully placed the candles in her pair of chandeliers in the front room. "Start of your first and last year at Forcastle College."

They had done well to get the house in order in just under a week, and that had been down to his mother's planning and his father's military execution.

"Your most important year thus far," added his father, who was relaxing on the heavy leather sofa in his hounds-tooth jacket, flicking through the papers. "Final exams at the end of it, if you're going to enter Plymouth College. It's now or never, my lad."

"And he's going to participate in the Twin Tors," said his mother. "Right, that's the last one," she announced triumphantly. "I'll let you do the honours, Chester - you're getting good at it."

Bentley picked up the box of matches from the table and waited for his mother to come down from the stepladder. He struck a match and began passing the flame round each of the candles. Once he had finished the first chandelier, he picked up the ladder and carried it through the archway into the other side of the room, where another elaborate chandelier hung.

"Wait a minute, Chester," said his mother, "you've missed a few."

"No, I haven't."

"I think you have."

"I lit them all."

"No, you've missed some," confirmed his father, joining the conversation without lifting his head from behind his newspaper.

"Really? That's impossible."

"Well, they must have blown out," said his mother.

Bentley returned and relit the offending candles. He waited a moment to make sure a draught didn't blow them out. No, they are fine, he thought.

He returned to the other side of the room to finish his job.

"You still haven't fixed them," said his father, his gaze still buried in his papers.

Bentley stomped across the room, "How on earth…" he huffed. Several of the candles had indeed gone out. He quickly returned with the stepladder and relit them. Then he stood back and waited. Slowly, one by one, some of the candles went out. One to the left, one to the right, one above him and one furthest from him. They're in completely random order, he thought. It's impossible for it to be a draught.

"Want me to do it for you, Chester?" said his mother.

"No, no. It's just—"

"Come on then," she interrupted. "As they say… the best man for the job, is a *wo*-man, isn't that right, dear?"

"Whatever you say, my pumpkin," replied his father, lifting his gaze briefly to grin at his son.

His mother climbed the two steps, lit the candles and then returned to reading *Country Life* on the sofa.

Bentley folded his arms, waiting for the inevitable to happen, but it didn't.

"Now you've seen how it's done, you can do the other one, can't you?" she said nonchalantly.

Bentley looked frustrated and dragged the stepladder back to the other chandelier for the third time.

He lit the candles as he had done before and joined his parents. He was just about to sit down when his father spoke, "Seem to be having the same problem with that one as well," he said, without turning his head to look at the far end of the room.

"Really, Chester," said his mother with slight annoyance, "I know you're tired from moving all the furniture around, but you could at least make the effort to light a few candles properly."

Bentley walked over to the chandelier and noted the candles, he was amazed. That couldn't be a coincidence, he thought. Or could it?

But before he could investigate further, his mother had pulled the stepladder out of his hand and was marching up it to fix the problem herself.

"There," she said, "and may that be the end of it. I have some serious reading to get on with."

Bentley just stayed where he was, looking up, but as before, the candles decided to behave themselves.

"Tell you what, Chester old boy, you couldn't fix us up a brew, could you?" asked his father.

Bentley sighed in resignation at yet another chore, and then his mother chipped in for good measure.

"Now do be sure to read the instructions on how to switch on the kettle."

"Thanks, Mother."

"Always here to help."

As Bentley disappeared from the room, his mind returned to the candles. There was something he would have to try later, if not, his mind would not rest. But he would have to do it when his parents were out of the house. If they saw what he was up to, they would think him quite mad, as anybody would if they knew what he was thinking.

- V -

THE HOE
Plymouth, 1588

The clear July sunshine fell generously across the gathering of men that amused themselves at sport on the sloping green ridge of Plymouth Hoe. A small group bent their backs and arms to a game of impromptu bowls, while others admired the deer that grazed nearby and a few stared in deliberation at the mythical limestone figures of Gogmagog and Corineous, cut into the hillside, doing battle. Would their encounter with the Spanish - some seemed to ponder - see them become the victorious Cornish hero of Corineous, smiting a fatal blow against a giant foe?

The rest of the men, their minds equally concerned with the war close at hand, gazed out across the natural harbour of Plymouth Sound, where a tall forest of masts bobbed restlessly as England's fleet lay in wait.

Never had so many vessels come together on British shores, and the forbidding sight had brought many of Plymouth's citizens out to witness it.

Then a ship was sighted. It approached the Sound, in full sail, interrupting the game of bowls. The men's hands instinctively fell upon the hilts of their swords, and a buzz of murmuring began.

"That is the *Golden Hinde* of Captain Thomas Flemyng," said John Hawkins, Her Majesty's Admiral of the Fleet. He marched down the green slope, where he found the High Admiral of England. "My Lord—"

"I am aware of the visitor," answered Lord Howard, stroking his distinguished silver beard, "see he is brought before us… and at good haste."

The air amongst the officers of the fleet had gone cold.

"Where is that cousin of yours?" asked Lord Howard, looking about, nervously.

"Ah… he is still playing bowls, I believe," answered Hawkins, in his Devon accent. There was further disgruntlement amongst the nobles.

"Bid him come hither."

"At once me Lord."

Hawkins signalled for a messenger to come forward, "See me cousin receives this."

The young messenger's eyes flared open when he realised he would have to meet the untamed sea dog face to face. "You'll find him here. You know where it is?"

The young man nodded.

"Good. Now fly. I will not be kept waitin' long."

As they waited for Drake to join them, a party marched up the slope.

"Captain Flemyng, I believe," said Lord Howard.

"My Lord."

"Well?"

"I have a sighting."

"We know," said Lord Howard.

They all turned to follow Lord Howard's line of sight and, beyond the estuary to Cornwall, where they saw the beacon freshly lit. They all stared at one another.

"Tell me what you have learnt then, Captain."

- VI -

A DANGEROUS WAGER
Plymouth, 1588

As Flemyng informed the High Admiral as to the state of the approaching Armada, a messenger jumped down from his snorting horse and disappeared inside a house.

Inside, the room was filled with smoke and men engaged in agitated conversation and boisterous activity. The messenger pushed his way through the melee of bodies and heard the great man before he saw him. He had not, however, seen the other man that had followed him into the building and hid himself amongst the crowd.

The intruder stroked his beard pensively and kept his head low as he followed the messenger. His darker complexion and more elaborate dress told the more observant man that he was not from these parts. What one could not have guessed though, was the underhand nature of his particular business.

A loud Devon voice boomed across the men and rolled across the wooden beams in the ceiling like a breaking wave. Then came the crash of wood, followed by hearty laughter and money feverishly exchanging hands.

The messenger tried to break through the impenetrable wall of men surrounding the famous sailor. One of them turned to see who was pushing him.

"What the hell does ye want, man?!"

"Message for Captain Drake from Admiral Hawkins."

"Why didn't ya say so?" The man turned round, but still did not allow the messenger to pass. "Francis!" he called out and the hive of activity that surrounded them came to an abrupt halt, causing a hushed silence to descend across the entire room. Even the pipe smoking slowed.

A man straightened up and the back of his head became visible for the first time to the messenger, who was then permitted to enter the tight circle of men.

"This littl'un has a message for you."

The messenger held up the scroll as Drake turned to look him in the eye. The mariner was a broad man as strong as a ship's mast. His gnarled hands bore the signs of a hard life at sea that had carried him to the ends of the Earth. And yet he was dressed in the greatest refinement, with a pearl earring, of significant worth, in his left ear.

Drake had confronted all of Spain, and feared no man, nor any monarch, and now the messenger was squarely before him.

The young lad began to feel the pressure. Drake looked deep into his eyes as he held his hand out courteously to take the parchment. As he did so he passed an object to the sturdy box-shaped man next to him. "Take this, Moses."

No one spoke. Drake tottered slightly, more stable at sea it seemed than on land.

"This had better be worth interruptin' me sport, lad," Drake winked kindly at the nervous young man.

He unfurled the document and his eyes flashed across the brief letter. Then he laughed quietly, "The Armada has arrived."

"We should leave for our ships," said one of the group and turned to get ready. Drake caught him by the arm.

"Where d'ya think you're goin', man? There is plenty of time to win this game, and to thrash the Spaniards too."

A roar of laughter rent the confined room.

18

"Anyways, the tide is not favourable and me head could do with the rest before battle." Drake sat down. "Fetch me some water. And you," he said, pointing at the messenger, "tell me cousin, and only me cousin, that the Vice-Admiral shall be along in good time." He shook his hand warmly before allowing him his leave.

"A wager then, Francis?" proposed his sparring partner.

"What d'ya mean?"

"We have yet to finish the game," said Percy.

"And?"

"One last shot, winner takes all."

"I'm up for that," said Drake joyfully.

"Not so fast Cap'n, if ya wins this one, then I say it is a sign that ya will take victory over the Spanish. But if ya loses, then victory will be theirs. What d'ya say now?"

The room fell understandably silent. The challenger was tempting fate, all sailors were superstitious men, any glimmer of hope to carry them safely across the devilish seas was to be welcomed, but there was no reason to provoke Providence.

"You're testin' me nerve, now are you? I'm not the superstitious sort."

The outsider that had been observing Drake, pressed forward and then he saw what he had come to see. Drake took a gold object from around his neck and kissed it. The onlooker tried to get closer to see exactly what it was. He had only ever heard stories about it, and desperately wanted to see it for himself, but for now he would have to bide his time. His chance would come once they set to sea, when every man would serve their own best interest.

"Why kiss it then?" taunted Percy.

There was a brief pause.

The small gathering could only stand in silence and mumble the same sentiment. They all felt that their fate was now literally in Drake's right hand, and the atmosphere was palpable.

The outsider moved closer again with the nervous shifting of bodies, keen to see Drake and keener still to see what was on the end of that gold chain.

"For England!" boomed Drake, "and to hell with you!" He turned and fired off his shot without hesitation. Within the same instant the room erupted in jubilation, as if Drake had sunk the Armada then and there.

Moses handed his master a mug of ale, which Drake drained in one as he received a volley of hands patting his back and broad shoulders.

Percy approached him and slapped the modest pouch of gold coin in his hand, smiling as he did so, "Ya old dog!"

"For England!" cheered Drake.

"For England!" his contingent roared.

It took some time before the feverish celebration subsided and the men could hear each other talk.

"What shall I do with this, Sir Francis?" asked Moses, looking down at the object Drake had given him.

"Keep it safe and mind you don't lose it, now. That is a good luck charm that just saved England, remember. I entrust it to you."

The outsider tried to get closer to see what Drake was doing with the lucky object, but a wall of men blocked his view.

"I thought ya said ya weren't superstitious?" joked Percy.

"I'm a sailor," Drake answered.

"But this is too valuable to take with us," said Moses.

"That is why I don't want it bein' lost here. It's as safe in your hands as anywhere else."

"Aye, aye, Cap'n," Moses tucked it away inside his tunic. Everyone watched him stow away the precious object that would carry England's future. Everyone that was, apart from the man who had come to spy on Drake, and who now left ahead of them before they became suspicious of his alien presence.

FORCASTLE COLLEGE
1981

Forcastle College stood amid the windswept moorland, doggedly resisting the relentless elements as it had done for over a century. Not far was the training ground of the Royal Marines, and nearer still was Dartmoor prison. The school was, therefore, well-positioned should any of its 'inmates' try to make their own way out if its imposing gates and strike out for home.

The pupils stood in line for the tuck shop, eager to get their chocolate, biscuits and crisps and then head down to the playground as soon as possible.

They all counted up their change to estimate what they could afford.

"Are you doing the Twin Tors this year?" asked Marina, but before anyone could answer, a sudden commotion broke out, as Adam Britton snatched someone's tuck money at the front of the queue. No one did anything.

"Shouldn't we get a teacher?" asked Carson.

"Come on," said Bentley. "You've been here long enough to know; nobody ever tells a teacher. The rest of the boys wouldn't respect you, they'd just laugh at you."

"That's the thing with you boys, you're all too willing to obey as if it's some kind of endurance test," added Marina. "Us girls speak out more often."

Bentley and Carson just looked at each other blankly.

Britton looked up to see Marina staring back.

"What are you staring at, 'Moses'?" he was always taunting Marina about being Jewish, ever since he said he saw her enter the city synagogue. She just laughed at him as usual. Britton didn't know what more to say and turned round.

"Aren't you going to do something?" said Bentley. "That's racist!"

"I know it is," replied Marina, who appeared unflustered. "But it's Britton, he doesn't know any different, he just repeats what he hears at home. Besides, aren't adults always telling us that 'sticks and stones will break our bones, but names will never hurt us?' And since when was being called Jewish a bad thing? They're one of the most resourceful people around. Look how they have transformed the desert?"

"I know, but you still have to tell one of the teachers," insisted Carson, "otherwise how will he ever learn what's right?"

"It's just a name, and there's more than one way of learning a lesson."

"But... but..." Bentley stuttered.

"But it's the hateful way he said it. He can't put you down for just being Jewish," added Carson. "You really should do something!"

"I will, don't worry, but now isn't the time. His name is Britton, isn't it?"

"What's that got to do with it?" asked Bentley.

"Everything. Revenge is a dish best served cold. You'll see."

And as there was no moving Marina on the subject, the other two gave in and let her have her way. Bentley and Carson looked at each other and shrugged as Marina glided off majestically to buy her crisps as if she knew something they didn't.

Bentley was glad to get home that evening.

"Good day at school, dear?" called his mother as he and his father entered the hall.

"Different."

"I should jolly well hope so, with the fees we're paying! Not even tax deductible, you know, and with all the money we're saving the State." Bentley let her blow off steam. "You wouldn't mind getting those candles going again, would you, Chester?" she called out to him from the kitchen. "Your father and I will be along shortly."

"*You* will," his father said to his wife. "You're the Baroque devotee. I have no desire to go blind before my time in that dim candlelight, thank you very much."

Bentley realised that this was his moment. He dumped his stuff on the monk seat and rushed into the living room. He swiped the matches off the mantelpiece, lifting the stepladder with the other hand as he went. He ran up it and lit the first chandelier and then stepped down to wait.

Just as he had predicted, the candles began to go out one by one. It gave him a slight shock at first, but he was determined to see it happen, eager to know he wasn't mad or incapable of lighting a few candles. Then he calmed himself and began to count. There were seven.

"Right, now the next one," he whispered to himself. He rushed to the other side of the room and repeated the same process on the other chandelier. The candles did the same thing. He held his breath when he counted them up. Seven candles left burning as well, he thought. That can't be a coincidence! And he was right.

That sealed it for Bentley, something was alive in the house. He had been trembling inside but now he broke out in a cold sweat. Seven? But what did it mean? He knew it was a lucky number in most cultures, but here it only felt like a curse.

Then he heard footsteps approaching and tried to react and get back up the stepladder, but he was too late.

"Still having trouble with those candles are we, Chester?" He was about to speak but his mother continued. "Oh, I see you've quite got the hang of it," and placed the bottle of Plymouth gin down beside the sofa. As she sat, she continued speaking, but strangely Bentley could no longer hear a word she was saying. Pressure had built in his ears and it made him feel giddy. But then his attention turned to his mother again who was still speaking, almost to herself, unaware of what was happening to her son. She seemed to be transforming. And then the horror came over him as he saw the most disturbing thing. Horns began to rise up out of her head. Bentley was fixed to the spot. His mother, however, was still oblivious to any of it. He thought he was going to explode and just as he was about to let out a scream, he heard her voice again.

"What are you going to play this evening for me dear? Something pensive I hope."

Bentley didn't respond - he couldn't.

"Chester? Chester? Are you quite all right? Chester!"

He snapped out of his thoughts the moment she shouted his name.

"Yes, s-sorry."

"I know you're a daydreamer, but you have to get out of the habit. I was asking for some music."

"Yes, of course," he replied as he got his breathing under control. He sat down at the piano. The music started up.

"Ah, Debussy's *Clair de Lune*," swooned his mother as she returned. "You read my mood entirely, Chester."

She sat down with her crystal tumbler in hand and watched Bentley at the piano. She closed her eyes as the music drifted out from the upright, rectangular piano and floated through the house.

Bentley stood up to walk out of the room, leaving the piano continuing to play of its own accord.

"Put it on repeat, would you? That's a dear," whispered his mother as she reclined back, the wood fire beginning to build its flames. Bentley turned and pressed the repeat button, next to the CD slot in the side of the automatic piano, where he had inserted the Debussy disc. The black and white keys continued to tinker away on the automatic piano.

He left the room quietly to let his mother rest, but he was a bundle of nerves. He had taken little more than a few steps into the hallway when the living room door slammed shut behind him. The noise boomed through the house. Bentley jumped and then his mother screamed. He flew to help her. The door wouldn't open. He rattled the handle, but it still wouldn't open. He could hear his mother whimpering. He was starting to panic but then the door opened by itself. Bentley rushed in.

"Oh, there you are!" blurted his mother, "what took you so long? Haven't you brought a cloth with you?"

"A cloth? B-but…" Bentley looked at his mother more closely and saw her cupping her hand. It was bleeding. He looked up to see if something had fallen from the chandelier.

"What are you staring at, Chester?" She motioned to a small table next to the sofa. "I cut myself on my tumbler." Bentley saw a spot of blood on a small jagged edge. His heart relaxed and began to beat more slowly.

He fetched a cloth from the kitchen and left his mother to convalesce. Bentley had more urgent matters to attend, he had some investigating to do. There was something paranormal in the house, of that that he was sure. And strangely, he felt an irresistible urge to discover what it wanted, as if he was being directed to do it by whatever it was that haunted the house. Nevertheless, he was still gripped by a potent and yet posssessive fear that now accompanied him wherever he went in the house.

- VIII -

WAR
Plymouth, 1588

Back on the Hoe, Lord Howard was growing impatient.

"Why has your cousin not been before me yet?" he asked. "I need his counsel, we are at war, Lord Hawkins."

"Aye, me Lord, I—"

"Ye came in on the tide, did ye not?" boomed a voice from behind them that sought to address Captain Flemyng directly. They turned to see Drake himself approach.

"Aye, Captain Drake," came Flemyng's equally direct answer.

"Then we are captive till the tide turns before nightfall."

"If the Duke of Medina Sidonia turns his fleet into the Sound, England will fall," contested Frobisher.

"He will engage in no such foolish act," countered Drake. "We have good knowledge that he will take the Duke of Parma's army to London. He has a south-westerly wind that will carry him to meet that army at Calais. He will not lose time with us, he does not have the gall to go against his King's command."

"Drake," interrupted Lord Howard, "We must still ready ourselves. If they dare enter the harbour, then our enterprise is ended."

"I have, aye, singed the King's beard, me Lord Howard," answered Drake, "but me razor is sharpened so as to shave his moustache and finish the matter between our nations this fine day."

There was a cheer from the men. Howard, High Admiral of England, fought a smile at Drake's insolent words.

Drake, the chancer, the relentless pirate and agile seadog, would carry the men with him, and they were eager to follow.

As they gathered their belongings and readied to make their way to the ships, the outsider who had so closely observed Drake and his gold possession, approached Drake.

"My Lord."

"Senhor Mendez," said Drake in high spirits.

"I must warn you that I have had word that King Philip's spies are amongst us."

"You are a suspicious one for a man of Portugal, I must say."

"Please," said Mendez, trying to lead Drake to one side out of earshot of the other men, "I believe your navigator is to be watched."

"Old Moses, ya say?"

Mendez did not flinch, but his eyes wandered to see if he could glimpse the chain around Drake's neck and better still the immeasurable treasure he imagined was at the end of it.

Drake bellowed with laughter, "He was me navigator around the world. I owe him me life as much as he owes me his."

"But he is Jewish, no?"

"And what has that to do with loyalty to England?"

"The Jews are not to be trusted, you know this?"

"Our Lord Saviour was *King* of the Jews, so you're sayin' he was not to be trusted either? Be gone with ye, Mendez. You're a fine sailor but ya make for naught when it comes to intrigue."

Mendez eyes lowered like a dejected dog.

"Moses!" called out Drake, and his trusty ship mate arrived at once. "Take this for me," and he handed him his sword. "I think ya'll find that is me answer, Senhor Mendez. I bid ya good day and a fair fight."

"Call the men to assemble!" cried Lord Howard of Effingham. Hostilities were about to commence. The cry went up and the captains and their immediate crew gathered to hear the High Admiral of England address them.

Lord Howard took the high ground on the Hoe with the thousands of crew before him, framed by Plymouth's natural harbour and England's amassed fleet. As he began his grand speech, seamen were already making their vessels ready for sail.

"Seafaring men of gracious and good England, the Pope, whom the Spanish have made their God on Earth, has procured King Philip and other potentates vassalled to the Pope, to invade this Realm, and to gain the Crown and country with the wealth therein to devour. Thus, the truth of all honourable actions now resides in the hazard to your lives, both in defence of her Majesty's person, and to the maintenance of this Crown, Kingdom, Country, and people, in the Kingly honour, and ancient liberty wherein it hath remained and been inhabited with people of mean English blood, more than these five hundred years! You fight this day to save this of England… For Elizabeth! And for England!"

"For Elizabeth! And for England!" cried the sailors, as the Monarch's name resounded across the Sound and to the nearby shores of Cornwall.

Drake then lifted his sword, giving the signal for the two men waiting for his command to light the Plymouth beacon. The fire grew quickly, fanning the flames of war.

- IX -

THE VINCIBLE ARMADA
1981

The door to the class opened and the pupils of 6B rose to their feet. In strode Mr Pendrift, the history teacher. His frowning eyes focused on his wooden chair and table, which were raised on a platform in front of a green-faced chalkboard. As he paced across the floorboards, he waved for the class to be seated on their benches.

The distinguished-looking man adjusted his half-moon reading spectacles as he peered over them to inspect the pupils for the first time. He took his register, opened it in front of him, scanned the class and ticked his list as he called out their names. He then adjusted his tie and stood up again. His thinning grey hair was tightly combed back, his face deeply lined by a lifetime dedicated to his passion of sailing. He wore his tweed jacket as if he had been born in it and his thick-soled brogues creaked in tune with the old floorboards.

"Now, we'll be looking at the Tudors."

There was a groan in the room. Bentley also groaned but he would soon change his tune as he was about to learn more than he had imagined. He would come to realise that Pendrift's classes would be the key he needed to unlock the mystery, which was gradually taking shape in his house.

"Now, now. You *might* enjoy it. But we'll start local, to make things a little more meaningful and then we can broaden our scope. So, who is Plymouth's most famous son?"

"Raleigh?" suggested Marina Hernan, her keen eyes as alert as ever and framed by shiny coal-black hair. She was the brightest in the school, academically, musically and artistically. Bentley stared a little longer than he should have; there was something different about her that intrigued him, apart from the fact that she seemed to be the only one to stand up to Britton. She turned round.

"What about Drake?" added Bentley, trying to deflect the situation. Marina smiled, leaving Bentley marginally less embarrassed.

"I would go with Drake," said Mr Pendrift, "even if he was from Tavistock, just 15 miles north from here. Second man in history to circumnavigate the globe; first captain to do the entire journey; responsible for much of the successful action carried out during the Armada. Can anyone tell me about a famous anecdote, concerning England's first slave trader and national hero?"

"The game of bowls," said Jane Werrington, flicking her rebellious gold curls from her eyes.

"And what is he claimed to have said?"

"Something about having time to finish his game and thrash the Spaniards," said Ed Stanton, straining his neck like the class giraffe that he was.

"Good enough - *There is plenty of time to win this game, and to thrash the Spaniards too*'. But did it actually happen as it has been passed down to us?"

"But everyone knows it happened," said Werrington.

"It is true that the more a lie is repeated, the sooner it is taken to be the truth, but it does not mean it is true. There is no evidence for Drake having said it. For example, the first known written source for this quote, I believe, does not appear until 1736, so can we trust that it is an authentic recounting of what actually happened? And why is this not more widely known? These are often the questions from history that we must all grapple with. There is, however, another, more plausible, explanation for the story of Drake playing bowls."

"What's that, sir?" asked an impatient Tuttle, who was toad-like but slightly more popular among his classmates.

"I will reveal the mystery all in good time, young man. Meanwhile, I would like you to think of alternative explanations to the famous legend. Back to the Tudors then, and as we are all Plymouthians here—"

"I'm not," blurted out Tuttle, sinking his head further down into the neck of his shirt and jacket collar.

The class laughed.

"Quite. Your Cornish complaint has been noted, master Tuttle. Now if I may continue, we should at the very least know the most relevant event in our local history, if not, what hope is there for us knowing anything beyond our own narrow borders? I am of course referring to one of the main events of the Tudor era, no less. Namely?" he threw the question out into the air above the pupils. "Plymouth and many of her men were at the heart of the matter?" he added, to give them a bit more help with the answer.

"The Armada, sir?"

"Quite, Miss Hernan." The master began to pace the length of the room. "I shall expect you *all* to take notes as we untangle this thorny issue."

Wendy Wilcove, at the front of the class, pulled out a biro and wrote the title, *The Spanish Armada*. She was nervous and spindly thin. Mr Pendrift looked down at her as if he had just found a mouldy sandwich in her desk.

"What in the name of Beelzebub is that ghastly thing?"

"My notebook, sir," she answered worriedly.

"No! That! In your hand!"

"A biro, sir?" unsure if that was what the horrified teacher could be referring to.

The class understood the problem at once.

"And are we to be using such heathen devices at this school?"

"No, sir."

"And why ever not?"

"Because… I don't know, sir."

"Well, it's no good you not knowing why you should or should not do something," Mr Pendrift turned to the class. "Can anyone answer for her?"

Wendy turned to see if anyone knew why on earth they could not use a biro.

"Because it is the work of the devil," said Bentley.

"Very true, Master Bentley and thank you for that, but on a more practical and earthly level if you please?"

"Because," Marina started to speak, "it's not as elegant as a fountain pen."

"Precisely. Now, where's yours, Miss Wilcove?"

"It's run out of ink."

"Can anyone… ah, thank you, Master Tuttle."

Tuttle pulled out a bottle of ink. Wendy dipped her pen into the liquid and operated a lever on the side of the pen, sucking up the midnight-blue substance. She thanked Tuttle and turned back to her notebook.

"Where's your blotting paper now?" asked an impatient Pendrift, keen to continue with the lesson.

"Here, sir," said Wendy, pulling out a piece of thick pink paper from her pocket. It was already marked with several blotches of dark ink.

"Right then, we will start by debunking some of the more popular myths surrounding the Armada, and that way you may gain an education. We'll commence with a name. The English called it the 'Invincible' Armada as a bit of propaganda at home to inflate their victory. The Spanish attended to their wounded very quickly when they returned, which tells us they considered defeat a likely outcome, given the complicated circumstances. The Spanish had always referred to it simply as the 'Enterprise'.

"Now, there were three Armadas in total. After the first failed attempt, the Spanish tried twice more. The English had a very light-hearted crack themselves at invading Spain, landing in La Coruña but were easily seen off. We don't seem to remember that do we? But if you ever go to the fair Galician town you will note that the impressive main square is called *María Pita*, after the woman who initiated the counter-attack, crying *"Those with honour, follow me!"* She is a local hero there, and the episode is well-known, far from forgotten. What other Armada myths can we dispel for you? Ah, yes - the motivations for the Spanish to attack?"

"Religious?" offered Marina.

"*Which* religions?"

"Christianity and…" she went blank.

"Just teasing," he said. "It was *only* Christianity that was involved - the religion had split, so on the face it, it would appear it was a Catholic-Protestant conflict, whereas in reality, it was something else."

"My father always says," Tuttle interrupted, "that religious war is one group saying 'my invisible friend is better than your invisible friend.'"

Mr Pendrift smiled wildly at the unexpected intervention. "Thank you for that enlightening point of view, Mr Tuttle, but it is steering us on an altogether different course."

"Religion is always an excuse," went on Mr Pendrift, "often masking the real issue at stake. In the case of the Armada, it was only a small piece of the equation, motivating the devout King Philip II of Spain. However, there were the other reasons why Spain would have wanted to invade England, such as trying to muscle in on the trade with the New World, which was being jealously guarded by the Spanish.

"And what conflict did that also lead to between England and Spain?"

Silence again.

"The King of Spain had contacted Queen Elizabeth to intervene and stop her native Englishmen from doing what, at sea against the Spanish treasure fleet?"

"Pirates!" said Burt.

"Piracy, to be grammatically correct," said Pendrift. "But I put it to you, would this be sufficient to warrant a full invasion, a complicated undertaking that could cripple a nation's finance's and jeopardise a monarch's authority, should the campaign go wrong?"

No one spoke.

"As far as I'm concerned, I *don't* think it was enough, and in the case of the Armada, we know that it was only a contributing factor, as was the religious aspect already mentioned. The English were supporting the rebellious Dutch at the time to throw off the Spanish 'yoke', which means control. Philip possessed the Netherlands and the Dutch were turning to Protestantism and away from the Roman Catholic Church, while at the same time, claiming independence. It was this final affront to Spanish hegemony in Europe that left Philip little option but to intervene and to neutralise England."

The class sat pensively for a moment and then the question Pendrift was waiting for arrived.

"Sir," said Bentley, "what does 'hegemony' mean?"

"Excellent, Bentley - the question on everyone's mind, and yet only you were inquisitive, or perhaps brave, enough to ask. It quite simply means 'domination of one group or person over another,' and is one word that historians often use, so you should all make a note of that." Pendrift turned and wrote it on the board.

"Now there is one piece of surprising trivia and that is Philip of Spain was actually the rightful king of England by, what is known in Latin as *jure uxoris*, which means 'by right of his wife'. He had married Mary I, sister of Elizabeth I. They had ruled as equals. So, there was that abiding factor as well, although to a much lesser extent.

"We shall close by tearing down one last myth. Many believe that with the defeat of the Armada the balance of power shifted from southern Europe to northern Europe; from Spain to England. But this is just not the case. Spain continued to prosper, landing as much as three times more gold and silver in the 1690s than any decade prior. The English failed to make a sizeable dent in the Spanish navy and despite the loss on the return journey, Spain's navy went on to greater strengths. The Spaniards would also remain the dominant sea power well into the 17th century; later to be superseded, not by the English, but by the Dutch. The Armada was also just *one* conflict in a series of battles of the Anglo-Spanish war, 1580-1604. In essence then, what is celebrated here is that England breathed a huge sigh of relief in escaping the very real threat and attempt at invasion from a far superior power."

Fountain pens scratched across notebooks as the pupils raced to note as much of Pendrift's explanation as they possibly could. Then several hands went up.

"There will be time for questions next time. I wish to end with this one last reflection and that is the emotional side, the human element of the story and its great tragedy. It doesn't take much to sense the appalling loss on the Spanish side. Around half the ships, some 65, never returned, leaving about 20,000 dead from a combination of sinking, wounds sustained in battle and those executed that had the misfortune to survive the shipwrecking and come ashore in Ireland. The English spared those that landed in England or Scotland but showed no mercy if they arrived in Ireland for fear of drumming up revolt there. One extremely brutal act was the torture and subsequent hanging of a sixteen-year-old Italian boy, Giovanni, who was the sole survivor of the wrecked *Santa María*. The majority on the Armada expedition, however, perished from starvation and disease."

One hand was still in the air.

"Make it quick, Bentley, people are eager to breathe some fresh air,"

"Sir, you said you would tell us the real story of Drake playing bowls."

"I did indeed, you're right. I had quite forgotten. Sadly, there is no time to go into it right now, but why would one want to ruin the suspense surrounding a good mystery? I will tell you all about it another time.

"Right, I am done. You have survived my onslaught admirably, now it is time for fresh victuals and supplies - break time. You may go to the tuck shop."

- X -

WORRYING SIGNS
1981

Sherlock charged on ahead through the crisp transparent river. The ripples flowed across to the branches hanging down into the water on the far side. Bentley picked up the wet ball on the small patch of sand, below the green riverbank, and tossed it into the air. The Jack Russell disappeared into the silver arch of water that he kicked up as he flung himself into the air to catch the projectile. He landed in the shallow water and charged back to his master to repeat the process. The dog's yapping echoed down the narrow, picturesque valley.

"Come on then," said his mother, "let's move along."

Bentley came back onto the muddy path with Sherlock in quick pursuit. His wellies squelched as he left the water while the sleeves of his wax jacket made a rasping sound as he swung them by his sides. Sherlock charged on ahead. They passed the weir that poured its pure water down into the whirlpool below. The sound of the falling water had a soothing effect on the ramblers as the river carried along on the next stage of its descent through tranquil Devon.

Bentley breathed in the earthy woodland air, but then he stopped dead in his tracks by the bizarre sight that met his eyes.

Bentley found his father acting strangely. He was standing in the middle of the path bent slightly over, brandishing his walking stick about, as he stared down at the forest path.

At first Bentley thought he might have been clearing leaves but then his arm movements seemed almost violent and he was grumbling to himself.

"Jarrod!" called Bentley's mother. "Jarrod!" she insisted.

"Y-yes, dear?" he snapped out of his hypnotic state, standing bolt upright, which was more in keeping with his nature. For a second it was clear that he didn't know where he was, as he tried to get his bearings and then he saw his wife.

"Ah, Kalla. There you are, been looking for you all over," he walked off to join her in conversation with a couple neither had met before.

Bentley started in the same direction and stopped where his father had been standing, then he saw it. Scratched out in the ground was a startling drawing. It seemed like two stars on either side of a squiggly line. Was that supposed to be water? He studied it for a while, not knowing why it trapped his attention so much. Was it because his father had just drawn it and had been acting so out of character, or was it something else?

That's it, he thought. I've seen this before, but where? Where? It started to bug him. He knew he wouldn't get it out of his mind until he could remember, but he just couldn't recall it. And so, defeated by the strange symbol, he decided to join his parents. He was confident though, that sooner or later he would come across it again and then he would be one step closer to connecting everything together and solving the baffling events that were occurring in his house.

When Bentley caught up with his parents, he immediately realised the topic of their conversation. Oh, not another conversation about dogs! he groaned and stood by his parents as Sherlock pulled at the leash, keen to sniff out the competition. Meanwhile, the four adults talked about their respective pets and avoided talking about themselves.

It's a religious sect, Bentley thought. He loved dogs but he didn't worship them.

"What is she?" asked Bentley's father, pointing down at the happy little fella.

"It's a *he* actually," the tone of annoyance in the woman's voice was evident to everyone.

"Ahem - quite, erm… that's what I meant."

There was a brief silence until the man opposite Bentley's father tried to recover the situation; he for one didn't want to miss an opportunity to talk about his dog, "He's a Field Spaniel."

"Beautiful," said Bentley's mother. "I don't think I've seen one before and as for that shade of chocolate brown, quite unique." Bentley's father bent down to stroke the dog and it growled. He jerked his hand away.

"He's never done that before," said the woman innocently, holding the dog on the leash.

"Adorable dogs, aren't they?" cooed Bentley's mother.

"Absolutely," replied the woman. "Very athletic. Wouldn't want anything smaller than a Field Spaniel mind, can't stand those snappy little types, you know, the Chihuahuas, Westies and what's that runt of a thing they use for going down fox holes, dear?"

"Oh, yes," said her husband, trying to think of the name.

"A Jack Russell?" offered Bentley's father.

"That's the critter," said the man, and then everyone looked down at Sherlock for the first time.

"Yes, well," blurted out the woman, trying to save face, "you know what I mean."

"No, actually… I don't," said Bentley's mother, who was just about to walk off.

"But…" said the man, back-peddling, "whatever dog you have, they *are* angels, aren't they?"

Bentley's mother's face lit up anew. "Can't do a thing wrong," she added. "Old Sherlock here is our baby, isn't he dear? Wouldn't know what to do without him."

Bentley's father looked a little uncomfortable at the 'baby' comparison.

Bentley took a paper and pen out of his jacket and sketched out the symbol his father had etched into the ground. Then he stared at it, annoyed with himself that he couldn't recall where he had seen it so recently. Was it in class?

"Well, of course, you're my *big* baby, aren't you?" she continued, turning to Bentley. "You know what I mean."

"No," said Bentley, putting the paper away, "I don't."

"Well, as you were saying," she turned back to the dog walkers as if Bentley hadn't spoken, and then flashed him a glance of annoyance, "they really can't put a paw wrong, always happy to see you, never moan, keep you company—"

"Great conversationalists," added Bentley, "always wash the dishes."

His father smiled but his mother didn't look amused.

"We hear you loud and clear," said the woman, and then her dog closed the gap between itself and Mr Bentley's trouser leg, but before the owner had time to react, a sparkling jet of warm urine rained down on his clean walking trousers.

"What the—" he screeched, hopping out of shot. He wiggled his leg as hard as possible to shake off the wetness.

"Oh, my word!" gasped Bentley's mother. Bentley covered his mouth to stop himself from bursting out laughing.

The dog's owners were completely unaffected, "Oh, Harry, you naughty boy," she said.

"He is a one, isn't he?" said the man.

Bentley's father had his back to them and was bent over, dabbing at the wetness with his handkerchief. "Damn it!" he mumbled.

"There's no need to react like that," said the woman. "He was just doing his business, you shouldn't have put your leg in the way."

"You what?!" replied Bentley's father gruffly.

"Quite, Jarrod," interrupted Bentley's mother. "It was all your own doing. Poor thing, you scared him... when he growled earlier. It was only his natural response."

"Have you all gone mad?"

"Remember where you are, Jarrod, there's no need to make a scene. I *do* apologise," she turned her attention from her husband and back to the couple. She bent down to stroke the spaniel. "You are a cutie, aren't you?" The canine lurched forward and nearly took off her nose.

Bentley's mother gave a shrill screech as she jerked her head away from the dog's approaching jaws.

"What a treasure," said the man, smiling oddly. "No need to kiss the lady," he giggled slightly. "Where are your manners?"

"Yes, well," said his wife, "it was nice meeting you and your..." she looked down at Sherlock and her expression changed.

"Same here," replied Bentley's mother.

Bentley was in stitches, while his father fumed angrily, holding his leg away from him to avoid the smell. And the odd couple continued on their way.

"Father," said Bentley, changing the subject, as they walked back to the car, "what was that picture you drew on the path back there?"

"What picture?"

"The one with the two stars and squiggly line."

"Fancy being Michelangelo now, do we?" giggled his mother.

"Chester, do you see me going around drawing things?"

"No, but—"

"Well, I am hardly likely to be doing it now when we're out for a walk."

"But I saw you do it."

"You may have seen me next to the Mona Lisa, but it doesn't mean I painted it. Anyway, enough of this nonsense. What I want to know is: are you ready for that bacon sandwich now, my boy?" he said rubbing his hands, as Chester and the dogs clambered into the back of the Trident green Land Rover.

Bentley had to admit defeat. He might not get his father to confess to drawing the symbol, but he knew it had been sketched for him to discover. But what was this new clue pointing him toward? He hoped he wouldn't have to wait long before he would see it again and work out its real significance.

XI

A CALL FOR HELP
1981

Back in the kitchen, the Bentleys' tradition of Sunday breakfast after their stroll in the woods was in full flow. Bacon was spitting under the grill, sliced brown bread was waiting to be filled and mugs of tea gently let off steam.

"Oh my God, Chester! You're not going to put ketchup in your bacon sandwich, are you?" said his mother as she spotted the bottle.

"Firstly, Mother it's a bacon butty and secondly, ketchup is essential."

"That is treachery," exclaimed his father, "all you need to do is to wipe the bread in dripping and all is right with the world." He marched out of the kitchen with a mug of tea in one hand and a plate brimming with sandwiches in the other.

"Right, I'll have toast and marmalade instead!" said Bentley crossly, heading to the toaster. "I wouldn't want to offend you!"

He stood with his back to his mother as he waited for the toast to finish, then took it out and threw it onto his plate. He was just about to butter it when he gasped.

"What is it, Chester?" said his mother. "Decided that bacon butties *without* ketchup are a better idea after all?"

Bentley didn't answer at first, he couldn't. All he could do was stare down at the piece of toast.

"M—Mother, do you see anything on the piece of toast?"

"What on earth are you on about now?" she said and then Bentley passed her the mysterious piece of toast. She peered down at it, "Oh yes! Isn't that a thing. It really does look like the number 18, doesn't it?" she handed it back to him. "Anyway, eat up. It'll be cold by the time you've finished."

She picked up her mug of tea that had been resting on the morning's newspaper and walked out to the living room. As she lifted her mug it left the time-old circular stain behind. Bentley started to butter his toast and then noticed something that made him stop. The tea-stained circle had a large number 18 in its centre. Then he looked at the newspaper on the counter top and there it was again in a news headline, *'18 Missing in Storm.'* Couldn't be! he thought. He carried on preparing his breakfast. Suddenly the calendar fell off the wall. He huffed, one more interruption to him finishing his toast. He bent down to pick it up. He looked at the front page of the calendar and his eyes fell on a day marked with a red star, it was the 18th September. Had there been a star marking that day the last time he looked? He was starting to doubt his memory and sanity. He looked around to see if anything else had changed in the kitchen or looked about to fall, move or do something strange.

He returned to his half-buttered toast, finished it and started to apply the marmalade. As he finally lifted the finished article to taste it, something caught his attention. The digital display of his Texas Instruments watch was running out of control. He pressed the button to halt the stopwatch, but it didn't respond. It wasn't the stopwatch that was racing forward, but the time display. He tried in frustration to stop it, but it would not respond. He took it off in panic and cast it to one side, his breathing moving as fast as the counting numbers. Just then the numbers ceased to change and there, staring back at him, was the new time of six o'clock - in the evening, eighteen hundred hours. He stood there motionless, waiting for something else to happen, but there was nothing but an unnatural silence that hung about him.

Bentley slowly picked up his watch but instead of putting it back on, he slipped it into his pocket and took his toast into the living room, looking all about him as he went, making sure nothing was following him.

"I'm thinking about getting another, Jarrod," Bentley's mother said as Bentley finished his toast.

"Really," replied his father, preparing himself for battle. "Well, that's fine by me."

"Really?"

"Why, of course. But the poop scoop duties will fall to you from now on."

"Oh, I don't think that's likely to happen."

"Exactly, that's why you getting a second dog is not likely to happen either," he said triumphantly, folding his paper to one side and giving his wife a steely smile. She was speechless and then Bentley chipped in.

"What is the phrase father always quotes by Bernard Shaw about dogs?"

"I don't think we need to be reminded of it right now, Chester," said his mother sternly.

"Something like dogs at one end are all teeth, and at the other end all shi—"

"Yes, thank you, Chester," interrupted his father.

His mother just stared at him as if he had said her baby was ugly.

"I'll just go and make some more toast," Bentley said retreating rapidly.

"That would be wise of you," said his father, "and timely. By the way, before you go, I just want to mention, before I forget, that we have a gardener starting soon, used to be here with the previous family. He seems a bit weird but has an excellent reputation, so just be prepared."

Bentley nodded and left for the kitchen.

He stared down into the toaster to see if the heating elements had a strange shape to them, but they looked normal. He dropped the bread in and depressed the lever, submerging the two slices into the heat. Moments later there was a metallic click and the toast jumped loosely in the mechanism. He plucked it out carefully then burnt his fingers and dropped the toast. The pieces fell onto the plate, scattering crumbs in all directions. And there it was! Clearer than before - the number 7. It couldn't be a coincidence, he thought. He looked inside the toaster again. Then he took out another slice of toast and inspected it closely. He looked back at the number and realised that it was in no way coincidental.

"What is going on here?" he whispered. First, there was that spooky incident with the candles blowing out and now there is this eerie occurrence with the numbers. He had no idea what it all meant. Is it some sort of message, maybe? he thought. He felt determined to find out.

But no matter how determined he might be there was no going to sleep easily that night, knowing that something ghostly was happening in the house.

XII

THE OLD CENTRAL LIBRARY
1981

Bentley put on his checkered pyjamas and went to brush his teeth. His bathroom was at the far end of the house and the only sounds were those made by him. There was no noise from passing traffic, nor the banging of doors from inconsiderate neighbours. Bentley was in a privileged cocoon. All sounds were his, and his alone.

As he went through the motions of cleaning his teeth, he began to feel as if something was watching him. And that something was behind him. His brushing slowly stopped but he couldn't turn round. Whatever it was, now began to close the gap and rise up. All Bentley could see in the reflection of the mirror was the outline of its head and two large horns that grew bigger as the thing grew nearer. He decided to make his move and confront it, his hands were rigid with fear and determination. He spun round but all he could see was an empty bathroom. He began to pant, and his body slumped over as he let his fear drain away. He turned to spit the paste into the washbasin and there he saw the two horns on his head again. He jumped back from the mirror, falling into a chair where his favourite teddy was sat. He grabbed it for protection. Just then his mother came into the room.

"What is all the racket about?" then she saw what he was holding for dear life, "And what the dickens are you doing at your age, hugging Paddington!

Bentley stared at the bear, who stared back at him equally speechless.

"I was just getting ready for bed," he got back on his feet.

"I saw the light on and thought you'd fallen asleep and left it on."

"Mum?"

She turned as she was leaving.

"What do— I know this sounds strange, but what do animal horns symbolize?"

"My word, that is a strange thing to be asking at this hour. You should be asleep."

"I'm serious."

"So am I. What do you think I am, a walking encyclopaedia? You need to look it up in the library."

"The library?" Bentley whispered as if he had never heard the word before. His mother looked at him. Bentley seemed engrossed in thought and no longer in taking the conversation any further.

"I'll switch off the light then," she said.

Bentley just sat in the middle of the bed. His mother waited one more second and then the room fell into darkness.

"Good night, dear."

"Night."

The next day at school, Bentley had asked Marina to accompany him to the library, and on Saturday the pair were now walking down the grey, rain-soaked hill to one of the few classical buildings left to Plymouth after the war.

"Okay, can you tell me now what we are going to track down in the library?" asked Marina, eager to know what all the mystery was about.

"Horns."

"Horns? What do you mean 'horns'? I thought you said it was something 'unbelievable'. If I had known that then I would have—"

"It *is* unbelievable, but you wouldn't believe me, if I just told you at school."

"I can't believe you've just wasted my entire Saturday morning," Marina scowled and resigned herself to her disappointment as she entered the building, leaving Bentley outside in the drizzle.

When he caught up with Marina, he found her standing in front of the librarian.

"I don't know," she said, addressing the adult, "you'll have to ask him. He's the brains of the operation."

"What's that?" said Bentley.

"What section?" asked the librarian.

Bentley was about to speak but swallowed his words the moment he looked at the librarian. She stood there grim and proper, her mouth turned down and her dark hair pulled tightly back. Her dark eyes penetrated Bentley's stare as she fixed his gaze from behind her monocle. Her stern appearance intimidated Bentley.

"Do you have— do you have a section on... Devil worship?" Bentley eventually asked.

"Devil what?" screeched Marina.

"You'll find that's under 'Satanism'," said the librarian matter-of-factly. "Follow me, please."

The librarian took off. Bentley and Marina had to fly to keep up with her.

"Satanism?" hissed Marina under her breath, trying not to draw attention from those quietly going about their reading.

"I told you it would be unbelievable. Are you glad you came now?"

"Have you gone mad?"

"Scared are you?"

"No. I don't believe in the Devil. I just don't want to get dragged into some crazy sect, or something."

They followed the librarian down a flight of cold granite steps into the dark and forbidding basement. She pushed through a heavy pair of doors, flipped the light switch and stood still. She waited while the lights all flickered into life, then she proceeded down the central aisle of the bunker-like room.

"Here you are," she said, stopping at a dark section in the furthest corner of the room from the entrance.

"Is this where you keep all the dangerous books?" asked an intrepid Marina, putting on a brave front, despite the spooky room and the librarian's scary aspect.

"No," frowned the woman, "those books are kept down there." She pointed at a section of a spiral staircase that disappeared into a sinister-looking trap door in the floor.

"What books do you keep down there?"

"You really don't want to know." And without any further explanation she disappeared.

"Right," said Marina, "now you've dragged me down here into the bowels of the earth, do you want to tell me what these horns are?"

"I keep… seeing images of horns in my house. It's really creepy, so I need to know what they mean."

"But why drag me into it? Maybe you're going mad."

"As I told you at school yesterday, who knows better than anyone how to hunt down information than you?"

"Bah!" she tried to shrug off the flattery, but she secretly liked it. It was true. She was rather good at finding the answers to obscure questions. She pushed past him, trying to suppress a smile and vanished into the murky aisle of books, many of which looked as if they had never been touched since the day they had arrived.

"Are you going to just stand there," she said, "or did you come here to help?"

Bentley walked into the cramped aisle and began scanning the books. There was a deathly silence, the only sound was dripping water.

"Horns… horns," he muttered as his eyes flew from one moth-eaten tome to another. A book suddenly crashed to the floor. Bentley and Marina jumped. It had come from somewhere near the entrance. They looked at each other, startled, but soon returned to their search. Then another book came crashing down to the floor. Marina lifted her hand and pointed across to a section by the entrance.

Together they edged their way to the source of the sounds. They peered round the end of a bookshelf and spied two books on the floor. Then it happened again, a book gradually crept out from its resting place and then toppled to the floor of its own accord.

"Oh my God!" said Marina. "Did you see that?"

Bentley could only nod. Marina slowly approached to investigate.

Bentley pointed at the sign on the aisle. Marina read the name of the section, "*The Occult*. What secret, hidden knowledge are we being led to?" he whispered.

Marina stared at the three books on the floor and bent down to inspect one of them, "*Mysteries of the Old Testament*." She picked up another and read the title also, "*The Resting Place of the Ark of the Covenant*."

"What's the connection?" asked Bentley.

Marina picked up the last book, "*The Truth behind the Death of Moses*. The connection seems to be Moses," she said.

"Moses? The prophet?"

"Apparently."

"And the horns?"

Marina picked up the book and started scanning the pages. "Look here, it says that horns have been associated with Moses, from *'having horns of light or rays of light coming from his head,'* in Saint Jerome's translation of the Old Testament into Latin."

On saying those words, a book began to wobble on the shelf next to them then it freed itself from the books on either side and slid out, falling to the floor. Marina stepped towards it and read the title, "*Mysteries of the Renaissance.*" Then the cover flipped open. Marina jumped back, her eyes wide with fear. The pages began to flick over in quick succession until they stopped, leaving a large image in clear view.

Bentley came closer and read the caption under the picture, "Statue of Moses by Michelangelo Buonarotti – in the Basilica of San Pietro in Vincoli, Rome."

"Look here, he has horns! It's true!"

Bentley was dumbstruck.

"So, Moses is contacting you."

"No, it doesn't make sense."

"The books fell off the shelf and opened on that page. You saw it."

"I know, I know, but it has to be some other Moses."

"What other Moses is there but the one from the Old Testament?"

Before Bentley had a chance to respond then the lights went out. They both let out a small yelp.

"Give me your hand," said Marina and the pair of them fumbled their way to the double door entrance. They pushed, but the doors were jammed shut. They pushed harder, starting to panic. Their breathing was becoming desperate and their pushing erratic. Then suddenly they screamed as the illuminated face of the librarian appeared right in front of them. A torch shed light from under her face, turning her grey face into a terrifying gargoyle. She waved her hand at the two children, telling them to move back from the doors. They stepped back and the librarian lifted a finger, gingerly pushing one of the doors toward them.

"You have to pull, not push, the doors," she said. "Did you find what you were looking for?"

The two children rushed out and carried on up the stairs to the light and into the street without so much as stopping to thank her.

XIII

DRAKE'S TREASURE
1981

Mr Pendrift waited outside the classroom while Troswell finished his lesson. The English teacher gathered his things and greeted Mr Pendrift as he walked out. The class noticed that the history teacher sailed in, blanking Troswell completely. The class stood up.

"As you were, ladies and gentlemen."

The class sat back down.

Mr Pendrift arranged his books, clasped his hands together and leaned back in his chair, considering his thoughts with the utmost care. "Where were we then?"

"Sir, is the Twin Tors as bad as everyone says it is?" asked Tuttle in the hope they could lead old Pendrift off the topic of class and onto his favourite subject of reminiscing.

"Nice try Tuttle," replied Mr. Pendrift, "but I think you'll find we were talking about the Armada. But for your information, the Twin Tors is far worse than people say it is."

Tuttle was doing the Twin Tors that year, as many of the class were, and now he wished he hadn't asked, as did the rest of the class, who stared at him, clearly annoyed at being reminded of their fate.

"So, we were discussing the Armada, but was that all?"

Wendy Wilcove's hand shot up, "Ah… ah no, sir. We also…"

Hands waved frantically, not giving poor Wendy a second to gather her floundering thoughts. Pendrift put her out of her suffering.

"Proceed, Werrington."

"Yes, sir. You talked about some of the myths surrounding the Armada."

"Much better."

Jane Werrington beamed at the praise but soon stopped smiling.

"But is that all?" the master raised his eyebrows and glanced around at the pupils. "Yes, Stanton?"

"Ah… I've forgotten, sir. Sorry, sir."

"Don't waste your energy holding up your hand for no reason. Bentley? You don't have your hand up, what do you have to add?"

"Sir?" Bentley snapped out of his daydreaming. He had been gazing out of the window at the bowl of sunlight that was filtering down through the dark clouds over Dartmoor. "Ahem, yes, sir, well…"

"Are you going to disappoint me as well, dear boy? It was enough that Stanton had no idea but—"

"You said you would tell us," began Bentley, bursting into voice, "what lies behind the anecdote of Drake's famous boast to finish his game of bowls and thrash the Spaniards."

Pendrift lurched forward, his chair legs crashing against the floorboards. "That's what I wanted to hear! Good, someone actually remembered the only mystery I put before you; the only intrigue. But I will not reveal all now. Suffice to say, though, that Drake was, apparently, not on the Hoe, but elsewhere - somewhere he shouldn't have been. Hence, the reason to divert people's attention and place the action squarely on the Hoe."

"Was he not playing bowls because the game hadn't been invented, sir?" asked a curious Tuttle.

"Now, I never said he *wasn't* playing bowls. No. I never said that at all. But to answer your question, bowls has been played in England since the end of the 13th century - a different form of what we are used to, granted. The lawn mower wasn't invented until 1830, invented in Britain you should know, so the civilised lawn variant was evidently not being practised, but there was still bowls of a nature.

Bentley's attention then began to drift off, as was to be expected, his daydreaming taking him over as he stared down at his textbook, open on a page about Sir Francis Drake.

"No - there is a small mystery surrounding this most famous of pre-battle anecdotes, so I will allow you all to dwell on it for a while longer. As Winnie-the-Pooh was want to say: *'Think, think!'* " and Pendrift tapped the side of his head, imitating the yellow bear, trying to concentrate.

Pendrift saw another hand go up, "Yes, Miss Hernan?"

"I heard that Drake hid a lot of treasure."

"Interesting diversion. It's not the main point of today's lesson, but we can explore that avenue."

"What? A buried treasure chest?" said Burt, alive with excitement. The others giggled.

"I'm sure, Master Burt, that you are not the only one enthused by tales of buried pirate treasure, but please curb your enthusiasm. It gets in the way of my lecturing."

Marina held her hand up again. Mr Pendrift nodded.

"I know about the Drake Jewel."

"Pray tell."

"Drake presented Queen Elizabeth I with a jewel, commemorating his famous circumnavigation. It was a jewel made up from rare materials obtained from either side of the globe. It consisted of enamelled gold, captured off the coast of Mexico and bore a ship made from an African diamond with an ebony hull."

"Very impressive description, Miss Hernan, but we have come to expect nothing less from you. I couldn't have explained it better myself. Anyone know of any other Drake treasure?"

"Drake's Drum," said Stanton.

"Very well, what can you tell us about Drake's Drum?"

"It's a… er… drum… and it belonged to Drake."

"Outstanding, Stanton, first-grade scholarship. I, for one, am unable to argue with such a concise definition."

"I think *I* remember something about it," said Bentley, "when I visited Buckfast Abbey recently."

"Whatever it is, it can't be much less than what Master Stanton has grasped."

"Well, it is a drum that Drake took with him on his circumnavigation of the world and then shortly before dying, requested it be left in Buckland Abbey. He said that should old England ever require his help, then they should beat upon the drum and he would come to the nation's rescue."

"Much improved. The Drum was moved to Buckfast Abbey after Buckland Abbey suffered fire damage. The drum on display is, in fact, a replica."

Bentley was still looking down at his textbook, the debate in class entering and leaving his consciousness, but something else was holding his attention, but he couldn't fathom it out. But whatever it was it seemed to be in front of him on the page staring back up at him.

"Where's the original, sir?" asked Wilcove.

"I think it's in storage along with other delicate national treasures, but I couldn't tell you where. I'm not an expert on Drake's Drum, but Professor Stanton here might know if you would like to consult his superior knowledge on the topic."

The class giggled while Stanton gave a blushed smile, shrugging his shoulders and stretching his arms under his desk.

"The drum is an important icon of English folklore, in fact, and is immersed in legend," continued Mr Pendrift. "People have heard it beating down through the ages. For example, when the *Mayflower* sailed from Plymouth for the New World in 1620, the drum was heard. Also, when Admiral Lord Nelson was made a freeman of Plymouth; when Napoleon was brought into Plymouth Harbour as a prisoner; and when World War I broke out in 1914 - to name but a few notorious incidents."

Bentley then saw it. It had been right under his nose and he hadn't seen it, until it wished to reveal itself to him and it jumped off the page and bit him.

"Isn't there supposed to be an actual Drake's treasure?" spoke up Marina.

"I was just coming to that, Miss Hernan, just coming to that. There is the legend of Drake burying a chest of treasure, part of the booty captured from the Spanish treasure ship *Nuestra Señora de la Concepción*, nicknamed *Cacafuego* - I will not translate it due to your delicate ears, when he landed in California and claimed it for England, under the name of *Nova Albion*, Latin for 'New England'. Some say near San Francisco."

The class was enthralled, nobody was looking out of the windows, prodding their neighbour with a compass or carving their initials into the desktop for posterity. They were all staring wide-eyed at Mr Pendrift and his ability to relay the tiniest of facts to illustrate his point and illuminate his stories.

"A treasure Drake caught closer to home, however, and over which there is no controversy was that of the pay ship *Nuestra Señora del Rosario* that Drake captured during the Armada. It had aboard a dozen chests of gold coin, tons of silver royals of plate and a handsome quantity of gold. The ship and its crew were taken to Torbay."

"There's hidden treasure in Torbay?" asked an amazed Tuttle.

"There's the 'Spanish Barn' of Torre Abbey in Torbay, where the captured Spanish crew were kept, but the coin and precious metals are well spent by now."

"What about Drake's sword, sir?" asked Burt.

"What do you mean?"

"Isn't it buried or something?"

"Or something, will have to be the answer to that. The whereabouts of Drake's sword has never been a mystery as it is kept in the Officers' Mess at HMS Drake, just down the road in Devonport Naval Base - biggest naval base in western Europe, I'll have you know. And the Queen, I think it was in '67, apparently used it to knight Francis Chichester, the first person to sail solo around the world."

Bentley's eyes focused properly now on the image in his textbook about Drake. He knew he had been looking at something important, but it looked so different that it had taken him time to realise what he was really looking at. Yes, it was the coat of arms of Drake, but it was only then that he understood that it was what his father had drawn on the path, when they had gone for a walk. Eureka! he thought, and read the Latin inscription that accompanied the coat of arms: *Sic Parvis Magna*. Am I being led to Drake? If so, what has Moses from the Bible got to do with it? It felt too crazy to believe and yet there was no mistaking the things he had witnessed, nor the repetitive nature of the symbols and mysterious goings on. Someone or something seemed desperate to contact him. It was as if it was their last chance. Time was running out.

There then came a knock at the door, and Mr Troswell walked in without saying a word to Mr Pendrift and addressed Bentley. "I haven't got your writing book." Bentley lifted the lid of his desk and began to rummage for it.

"Master Bentley," said Mr Pendrift in an uncommonly cold voice, "I do not remember telling you to open your desk while I am still teaching."

"It's just a minute," said Troswell, "I won't—"

"How convenient for you," said Pendrift addressing Troswell, but kept his eyes on the pupils. "I will continue my class despite this uncalled-for interruption. The exit door is from whence you came, Mr Troswell and where you shall go thither, this instant. And the next time you require a student's book, I sincerely suggest you organise yourself more appropriately, so as not to barge into anyone else's classroom. Good day to you."

"Mr. Pendrift I only wanted to—"

"I *said* good day, Mr Troswell."

Troswell sunk back toward the door, reddened and intellectually beaten. He was the English teacher, but it was clear to everyone that Pendrift had a stronger command of the language than he did.

As soon as Troswell closed the door, the bell rang and class was over.

"Perfect timing," said Pendrift and began to whistle a tuneful melody as he collected up his books.

- XIV -

A BUMP IN THE NIGHT
1981

Bentley stood at the sink, cleaning the grease out of the drip tray where they had grilled the bacon, after another beautiful stroll along the river. His father sat, like most Sunday mornings, in the front room, his nose buried in the *Financial Times,* searching, as he would say, for 'the next big thing'.

Next to Bentley, his mother had laid out the snow-white dough she had been working on in three slender strips that were about to go into the oven. She turned to clean the work surface and then turned back, when she gave an unexpected shriek, "Chester! That's enough of your childish games!" Bentley looked over to see what the fuss was about and then he saw it too - the strips of dough had been interlaced.

"But *I* didn't do it," he said in his defence.

"Ha, ha. Very funny."

"No, really."

"And I'm supposed to believe that? Pull the other one it's got bells on it."

Bentley lifted his hands out of the sink to reveal a pair of pink rubber gloves covered in water, detergent and pig fat.

"And what's that supposed to mean?" she asked, as she set about untwining the bread.

"How am I supposed to have done that, if I have my—"

"I'm not interested in any more excuses," she cut him off, "just don't do it again. Look at this mess, I have to start again."

Bentley gave a small huff in desperation and continued to clean the grill pan, while his mother separated the strands of dough and rolled them out neatly once more.

"They've stretched. I'll have to do baguettes now, instead of rolls. Oh well, never mind."

Once done, she dusted them lightly with some flour and turned round to clear up. She looked back just seconds later and screamed, "Chester!"

Bentley lifted his hands out from the soap suds in the sink, "Not me this time either."

"Well, well…" huffed his mother trying to gather her thoughts. "You… you can… cook it yourself!" As she stormed out of the kitchen, the oven pinged that the correct temperature had been reached.

Bentley was also a little shaken, but more than that intrigued at this latest sign. He took off his gloves and studied the entwined pastry more carefully, before sliding the baking tray into the oven. What did this latest clue mean? He was getting more confused. Was something about to happen and he was being warned?

"Finally, you've managed to get the hang of those candles," said his mother, as she fixed her hair in the hallway mirror that evening. Bentley peered into the front room and looked up at the chandelier he had lit an hour before. All the candles were still aglow.

His parents fussed over their final details, fixing a tie and tying a scarf.

"We won't be long, Chester dear. Just a quick dinner with the Clarkes and then we'll be home," said his mother, popping a lipstick into her bag.

"Yes, you've got the number, son, should you need us," added his father, patting him on the shoulder. "And you've got Sherlock to protect you, should things come to the worst."

"What a ghastly thing to say," said his mother.

"I wasn't trying to scare him."

"I didn't mean *that*, I meant that poor old Sherlock would have to tackle a burglar. He might get hurt." She turned to look at her son, "Just use the shotgun, dear. You can't miss that way. And make sure Sherlock is behind you when the thing goes off."

Bentley's father raised his eyes to the heavens, as his wife sailed past him and out through the white doors. Bentley grinned at his father, who winked back and then closed the doors behind him.

The car engine rumbled and then it was gone. The house suddenly became alive with silence and Bentley began to hear things he had never heard before.

The wellington boots now stood dry in the boot room beneath a heap of wax jackets and dog leads. Night stars floated above the skylight, shedding silver strands of light down into the dimly lit hallway below. Old furniture creaked and the wind whistled lightly down the numerous chimney stacks, dotted throughout the long building. The only things that moved were Bentley's lungs, Sherlock's nose and the pendulum on the grandfather clock.

Bentley stood in the faded light of the hallway, listening to everything. Then he looked back at the chandelier through the doorway and the candles blew out, one by one, leaving just… *seven* lit. It was then he thought of Sherlock, *where was he?* A dull thud came from one of the two front bedrooms upstairs. He didn't want to, but he felt drawn to go up and investigate. He walked up the winding staircase and arrived on the first landing then looked up at the main landing with its five doors. Two on the right went into the front bedrooms and the three on the left led to two more bedrooms and a bathroom. He couldn't hear anything distinct, but he could swear he sensed a presence emanating from his parents' master bedroom. He looked above him at the night sky through the skylight. It was a beautiful night, all was well, he thought and then he heard a noise from within the bedroom and cold sweat erupted all over him.

Slowly, he walked up the rest of the stairs, keeping his back to the wall, ensuring nothing could creep up on him. He went to the first bedroom door and opened it. He held his breath as he jumped into the room, trying to be brave, and scanned the space. There was nothing there. He closed the door behind him. Now he edged his way cautiously to his parents' bedroom door and was just about to place his hand on the knob when it rattled. He removed his hand as if scalded by boiling water and fell back against the set of drawers behind him, nearly knocking the wall mirror to the floor. He turned quickly to steady it and then looked back to observe the door knob. He was dripping sweat but there was silence on the other side of the door. He was just about to open it when he suddenly remembered that he could turn the landing light on. He flicked the switch and warm light bathed the space. At once he felt a whole lot better. He wiped the sweat from his forehead and confidently opened the door. Before he had time to react, something jumped out from the darkness and went straight for his face. Bentley gave a childish, almost primitive, squeal as he tried to shield his eyes, collapsing on the floor from the fright. But there was no getting the thing off him as it bared its teeth and lathered his cheeks with salivary kisses.

"Agh! Agh!… Sherlock!! What the— I could kill you!"

The dog looked as if he had been reunited with his master after a lifetime of separation. As Bentley managed to pull himself together and get up from the floor, he noticed the unusually thick door frame. Odd, he thought.

As he began to walk back downstairs, the bedroom door slammed shut, and Bentley started sweating again.

For a moment he thought of rushing back upstairs and confronting whatever it was that resided in the room, but his brief moment of bravery had passed and he would have to pluck up the courage another day.

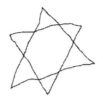

FAMILY SECRETS
1981

Bentley plonked himself down on one of the benches overlooking the rugby pitch and unwrapped a sandwich.

"Challah," said Marina.

"Say what?" asked Burt.

"Challah bread," she said, pointing down at Bentley's sandwich that his mother had baked him.

"And what sort of bread is that?" he asked.

"It's Jewish bread - normally sweet."

"And how do you know that?" asked Wendy.

"I'm Jewish, *aren't I?* " Marina gave a quick, sarcastic smile. Bentley caught it but didn't know what she meant by it. "When did you make it?" she asked.

"Sunday," but Bentley didn't have the courage to tell them it had interlaced itself.

"Oh, well, you're definitely not Jewish then," Marina told Bentley.

"What makes you say that?" asked Wendy.

"Challah bread is traditionally made and eaten on the Sabbath, which is Saturday."

Bentley fell silent.

"What is it, Bentley?" asked Burt, who noticed his friend's odd change of manner.

"Nothing - it's just my hand," but he was lying, he was thinking over what Marina had just said.

"For a moment I thought it was something serious," said Burt.

But Bentley wasn't listening, instead he was lost in thought. Something Marina had said made something click in his brain and he felt as if he was now one step closer to understanding the mysterious goings on at his house.

The drive back across Dartmoor and into Plymouth was pleasant as always after school, but Bentley sensed his mother's changed mood.

"Is there anything the matter?" he asked her.

"Your father will tell you when we get home."

"Am I in trouble for something?"

"Oh, no. Nothing like that. You have no need to worry," but that was not the expression she had on her face. Bentley asked no further questions. Something had happened at home.

The car pulled into the driveway and Bentley and his mother entered the hall together.

"In here," called his father. He was in the living room and put down the newspaper as they entered.

"Take a seat, Chester."

His mother sat next to his father.

"Listen, son," he said, "I don't want you to worry or anything, but Mrs Gardener, the cleaning lady, will no longer be coming here."

"We had an incident with Sherlock," said his mother.

"He pooped on the carpet again?" asked Bentley.

"What do you mean *again?*" asked his surprised mother.

His father flashed him a stern look, as if to say, 'that was our secret.'

"No, it's not that, Chester," interrupted his father, "he… apparently, snapped at her and as a result, she no longer wishes to come. That's all."

Bentley breathed a huge sigh of relief. "Phew, for a moment I thought someone had died."

His mother jumped at his words, "What on earth do you mean by that?"

"You looked so serious in the car, saying father had to tell me something. Now I know what it is, you could have just told me on the way back and saved all the stress."

"Yes," she tutted, "but your father has a much better way with words."

But there was something about his father's story and the way he had told it that didn't add up. Sherlock had never hurt anyone, and Mrs Gardener had always beamed each time she had seen him. Something else had clearly happened and he wasn't being told the truth. Why all the secrecy? And what did it have to do with Mrs Gardener?

"Listen, son," said his father, "to take your mind off things, here's my Minolta camera. I know you jump at the chance to use it, so we need some snaps of the house to send to your grandparents so they can see the new place. They won't be down from Weymouth for a while and that's the only way they're going to see the new house. I'll get the photos developed and sent off later this week."

His father never wasted time when it came to getting things done. As far as he was concerned 'why put off doing something tomorrow when you could do it the day before.'

Bentley took the camera and started where he was in the living room. "Oh, and remember," his father said as he was leaving with Bentley's mother, "the roll of film in it only has 24 shots, so use them wisely and don't waste a single one if you can."

"If they could only invent a camera that could take a hundred photos and then you could just see which the good ones were before getting them developed. You'd save a fortune in wasted photos," said Bentley.

"Not in your lifetime, Chester," said his father, "that's for sure."

Bentley finished up in the living room and then went out to the garden. He had just stepped out of the back door when he saw someone stand up with shears in his hands.

"Hello," said Bentley, not expecting to find anyone in the garden. The man just stared at him from beneath the long dark strands of hair that hung over his face, like the branches of a weeping willow.

Bentley froze for a moment when he realised the man was not going to reply and noted the cold hostility. Bentley looked down at the camera and went off to photograph the garden, but he could not think of anything except the bizarre encounter with the gardener. His father was right, he was strange. Hadn't he seen him from somewhere before? Something was clearly not right.

Bentley walked out through the large iron gates guarding the imposing row of Victorian houses, the rain streaming down his umbrella in beaded strands. He jumped over the water rushing down the leafy main road on its way toward the city centre at the bottom of the hill. He then carried on up the road and turned down into the secluded cul-de-sac.

The lines of neat rose bushes stood guard along the row of pre-war houses that sat calmly in their hidden and peaceful location. Bentley reached the end of the low garden wall in front of his nan's house, his shoes beginning to squelch from the intruding water.

He strode up the short path to his favourite front door and was just about to knock when it opened of its own accord. Bentley smiled, it would often do that. He propped his glossy umbrella in the stand inside the modest porch and left his dripping shoes on the checkered tiled floor. He pushed open the wooden door, its frosted glass pane rattling as he entered a world where father time had stood still, encapsulating an England of yesteryear. The digital era may have been dawning but here the analogue charm and craftsmanship of the nineteen fifties had remained intact within the four walls of his nan's prim dwelling.

He stepped into the carpeted hall and heard the pendulum clock chiming. To his right, the kitchen with its iron-cast Aga cooker was silent but warm. He glimpsed the vibrant red velvet wallpaper in the dining room and then he spotted someone moving about in the garden. He walked into the sunny living room, where the familiar music of the Royal Marines marching band floated out from the imposing gramophone cabinet, whose wooden lid was open like a giant jaw. In the garden he saw his nan tending her prized roses.

"Hello, Chester," she said and continued with her pruning.

Bentley descended the two steps and found himself in a foreign world of blue skies, mild insect humming and bright sunlight. He looked back over the roof and saw the dark clouds on the other side. His nan stood up and smiled at him but then she noticed his clothes.

"My word! Did you fall in the pond?"

"How could I do that if the goldfish pond is behind you and I have just entered the garden?"

"That's no excuse, you should be more careful," she answered in a fluster.

"But, Nan it's rain—"

"Inside then and dry yourself off."

She took him by the arm and led him back inside. Bentley sat in the heavy green, prickly sofa, making an effort not to disrupt the perfectly placed floral lace covers. His nan soon returned with a flowery towel for him.

"I'll just get some tea, shall I?" but before he could reply she was gone.

He looked down at the floral pattern on the carpet, the irises in the wallpaper, the roses on the curtains and the collection of flower-themed figurines in the mahogany display cabinet. Before he could consider why there was so much floral overkill, a trolley appeared in the room, bringing with it a symphony of colour in the cake-stand and the percussion of reverberating porcelain china.

Nan poured while Bentley tucked in.

Once he had finished eating his fill of scones, jam and clotted cream, he asked what he had come to discover, "Nan, have you noticed anything odd about the house?"

"Well, it does creak a bit when the wind gets about it."

"No, I mean odd as in…" he couldn't quite finish the sentence.

"Oh… I think I see what you mean," she fell silent as she sipped her tea, considering whether she should say something or not.

"Well?" insisted Bentley.

"Yes."

"Yes, what?" There was a pause as she gathered her thoughts. Bentley's mouth went dry as she was about to answer.

- XVI -

FIRST ENCOUNTERS
1981

"Yes, I *have* noticed something odd as you say, but your mother should not catch us discussing such things," she sipped her tea again, "I was in the living room, hoovering, when I could swear I felt someone watching me. I turned round and there it was, in the entrance."

"What was it, Nan? What did you see?"

"Well, it went as soon as it had appeared, so I couldn't really say what I saw, but there was something there all right, of that I am sure."

"What if you're imagining it?"

"That's not what Mrs Gardener said."

"What do you mean? She left because Sherlock attacked her."

"Is that the case? And who, might I ask, told you that?"

"Father."

"Did he now? Well, Mrs Gardener, for your information, left, and this is strictly between you and me," she winked at him, Bentley crossed his heart, "because she saw what I saw. And not just the once, but on several occasions, come to think of it. After that, she gave up. She said her heart couldn't take it anymore."

"So my parents lied to me about the dog!"

"Just think of it as Father Christmas: it was a white lie. They didn't want you to get worried."

"Father Christmas never worried me," he said.

"Frankly, I don't know why children aren't terrified of stories of a grown man invading their house after midnight." Then there was silence between them.

"I think it's up to you," she said eventually.

"To do what?"

"To contact whatever it is that is in your house?"

"Why should I *want* to contact it?"

His nan put her cup and saucer down. "Chester, I have never told you this, and you must swear not to tell anyone what I am about to tell you, especially your mother. She does not like to hear such things, she believes it's all superstitious nonsense. But we know better now, don't we Chester?"

Bentley couldn't move his head to nod in agreement. He just sat there frozen, waiting to hear what unbelievable thing his nan would utter next. He had never seen her like this, like someone that had just been touched by madness.

"You have a gift, my dear. A gift for seeing things, for perceiving things that others do not."

"What things?"

"I don't want to tell you too much. I don't want wish to scare you, but you'll get used to it with time. We can see beyond the light, you and me, and through to the other side. There are only a few of us with such a talent. But you'll have to be careful how you use it."

"But I don't know what you're on about, Nan."

"You have a guardian angel watching over you. A jeweller, I think. You helped him in some way, it appears, and one good turn deserves another. He told me as much, and he will ensure you are blessed with the gift of serendipity, whenever you need it."

"Seren— what?"

"Serendipity, to make unexpected, but fortunate discoveries. Don't sound surprised. We all have hidden talents, some are more hidden than others. You will find out soon enough when you contact it."

"Who said I was going to contact anything?" his frustration was beginning to mount.

"You seem to have no choice in the matter. *It* has chosen *you*. And only *you* will do."

"And why me? What have I done?"

"Nothing yet. But you could go on and do a great deal. We shall have to wait and see how things develop. But it feels as if something is just around the corner. I'm so excited for you!"

Bentley didn't know whether to be excited too or completely terrified.

"Once, in the hallway, it nearly showed itself," she continued, "maybe it mistook me for you. Who knows?"

"B-but—"

"No buts, Chester. Just pass me the clotted cream, there's a dear." He did as he was told. "Oh, and one last thing," she said, "the real oddity is that Mrs Gardener and I both agreed that strange things happened when the dog was out of the house and never when he was at home. Curious that."

"But—"

She held up her hand not to be interrupted as she sank her false teeth into the reassuring layer of luxuriant clotted cream and let out a small sigh of delight.

When Bentley returned home late that evening, his parents were in the living room; seven candles were burning menacingly in the chandelier. He joined them on the sofa.

"We're looking through those photos you took of the house, Chester," said his mother.

"You managed to get some of them in focus this time," joked his father and passed the packet of photos to him.

Bentley didn't really want to spend any time browsing through the photos, but he had only got past the first two images when his expression froze. He stopped listening to his parents and lifted the photo closer, squinting his eyes. Is that what I think it is? he thought.

All sorts of explanations whizzed through his mind as he tried to find a logical explanation for the eerie looking symbol that lit up the corner of the mirror, caught in one of the first photos he took of the front room. Bentley could clearly see himself in the reflection, holding up the camera as the flash lit up the image.

"What does that look like to you, Father?" he passed him the photo.

"What am I supposed to be looking at?"

Bentley pointed to something on the right of the image.

"A trick of the light I suppose."

"But what does it look like?"

Before his father could answer, his mother took it from his hands.

"Looks like the Star of David to me," she said.

"That's what I was about to say… if I had been given the chance," he said in annoyance.

"Oh, don't get grumpy, dear."

"Do you think it's a trick of the light?" asked Bentley.

"Can't be anything else," his mother answered. "I mean look at it, it's a reddish squiggly line. Must be something to do with the camera flashlight."

"Let me take a look at that again," his father insisted.

Bentley returned it to him.

"Mmm," he mused, "must be the flash playing tricks, but it certainly looks like the Star of David, all right."

Bentley should have felt reassured, but something was telling him it wasn't the flash that had created the strange symbol in the photo.

"Right, I'm off to bed," said his mother. "Sounds as if a storm's brewing." Thunder grumbled its approach from a distance.

"I'll join you," added his father. "I'll just do the rounds and make sure everything is locked up while you see to the candles, Chester."

Bentley went to get a stool and put the candles out. He only had a few left to do when his father appeared at the doorway.

"I'm going up now, so if you're done here just make sure you switch off the rest of the lights. Goodnight, son."

"Night, Father."

Bentley waited for his father to close his bedroom door upstairs before he jumped down from the stool to take another look at the rest of the photos. There was nothing else that seemed out of place, so he went back to the photo with the inexplicable fiery Star of David in the mirror. He then looked up from the photo at the mirror, half-expecting to see something - but nothing was there.

He stood up to finish the candles and as he squeezed the last flickering flame with his wet fingers the room was swallowed up in darkness.

Damn it! he thought, I forgot to switch on the living room lights first.

He stepped down and as his foot touched the floor, he heard footsteps coming down the staircase. From the timing of the footsteps, he could tell it wasn't either of his parents. A sudden flash of lightning came from outside. He was gripped with terror. He couldn't lift his feet to carry him into hiding. Despite feeling the need to hide, he was possessed by a greater compulsion to stay and see what it was, as if pulled by some magnetic force.

The steps came further and further down the stairs. Bentley had begun to sweat and was now holding his breath. Just as the footsteps were about to turn and enter the living room and find Bentley, they went in the opposite direction and into the dining room and the adjoining kitchen.

Bentley recovered some strength and crept into the hallway, then he glimpsed something moving in the darkness, but it just disappeared into the dining room. He moved quicker to get a better look at whatever it was. He crossed the hallway and rushed into the dining room, but he was a fraction late again, as all he saw in the dim light was the side door to his left, creaking closed.

Bentley gathered his courage and went after whatever it was. He grabbed the door just as it closed completely and switched on the light. Then in a burst of frenzied bravery, he lunged into the corridor and screamed, "Aagh!!" bracing himself for the horrifying encounter. He stared down the narrow passageway, his head dizzy with dread and his pulse racing out of control - but the room was empty. Bentley stayed a moment to listen for any signs of movement, but everything had fallen silent. He turned round, back into the dining room.

"Aagh!!" he yelled at the top of his lungs, throwing himself backwards and against the wall in the corridor.

"Aagh!!" came the scream back at him. "What in the devil are you still doing down here?!" hissed his father, recovering from the fright. "I thought there was a burglar down here."

"No, it's me," said Bentley, his chest heaving as he tried to regain his breath. His father switched on the light.

"Well, don't make a habit of creeping about in the dark."

"I won't," said Bentley, as he bid his father goodnight again and walked out to his room at the back of the house.

As he went though, he was completely unaware of the dark figure, watching him from the cover of the night out in the garden, muttering to themselves, "It's mine, it's mine."

- XVII -

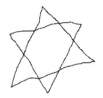

SEEING IS BELIEVING
1982

"We're just popping out to the Athenaeum, dear."

Bentley looked blankly at his mother.

"You know," she said, "the theatre?"

"They're playing Agatha Christie's *The Mousetrap*," said his father. "I won't ruin it by telling your mother the teacher did it." He nudged her in the ribs jokingly as she began to look disappointed, thinking that he had just ruined the ending.

"Only kidding, there's no teacher in it," he reassured her.

"Shall we be off, before I change my mind?" Bentley's mother pecked him on the cheek as his father patted him gently on the back, following his wife to the car, her heels clicking across the black and white tiles.

The moment the front door closed, shutting the rain out, Bentley turned and went into the living room, "Sherlock? Oh Sherrrrr-lock?" he called out to his faithful dog. The Jack Russell soon appeared, his ears pricked up curious to know if there was a treat on offer. Bentley scooped him up and carried him to the back door, where he unceremoniously dumped him into the cold night drizzle.

Bentley had something that he was determined to do that evening. He didn't want to think about it; he didn't dare. He just wanted to get it over with as quickly as possible - because tonight he was going to confront a ghost.

He walked back into the hallway, his palms already sweating with nervous anticipation. It's now or never, he thought. His parents and the dog were out of the way, which meant that tonight there was an above average chance that he would see it. That's what his nan had said, that both she and Mrs Gardener had seen it, when the house had been empty. That was, of course, if there really was anything to see.

He steadied his shaking legs and listened for footsteps. The house remained silent. He swivelled his head round to try and pick up the faintest of intentional sounds, but there was nothing. There was only one thing for him to do and that was to go after it himself.

He slowly made his way up the stairs and when he reached the top he stopped to listen again, but there was still nothing. He approached his parents' bedroom door, took one short breath and turned the knob. It didn't move. He knew he was onto something. He tried again, but it wouldn't budge.

He had psyched himself into a state where he believed he could take on anything, but he could go no further and his momentary courage rapidly left him.

He took a step back toward the top of the stairs, when he heard it - a sound, a disturbing sound. He turned. It had come from inside his parents' bedroom. He listened carefully. There it was again. A jolt of fear shot down his spine. It was… sobbing - it was a man. He found himself being drawn to it as if drawn to the imminent danger of a cliff edge.

He clasped the doorknob again, the sobbing continued inside. Bentley held his breath and applied pressure. The doorknob turned. As the door creaked open, the heavy crying ceased at once. Bentley pushed the door fully open now, his head dizzy, his heart beating frantically. His eyes scanned the room from right to left as his lungs reached bursting point, preparing himself for the horror he was about to see.

His attention was drawn automatically to the window and there… there was nothing.

Bentley marched bravely up to the armchair that faced the window with its view of the sea. He sensed that something had been sitting in it. It creaked as it gradually regained its former shape. A weight had evidently been lifted from it the moment he had entered the room.

Then Bentley heard footsteps, receding down the staircase. He rushed out and peered over the banister. He could swear he had just seen something move out of sight towards the bottom of the stairs. It looked like... a foot?

He careered down the staircase and flew into the living room, expecting to confront the thing, but he only saw the door leading into the corridor behind the dining room start to close. He leapt across the room and got his hand to the door just as it shut. He was too late again.

He opened it and thrust his head round the corner, peering down the dark corridor, only to glimpse something disappearing into the solid floor. But what was that?

"No, no!" he whispered to himself. "It can't have disappeared again!" He looked around the long narrow corridor and then noticed an old hook that he hadn't seen before, high up on the wall. Beside it was a strange little metal door. They looked as old as the house, and both were covered in layers of ageing white paint. They had clearly not been used for quite some time. Bentley had no idea what they were for. He needed a bit of help. He was at a dead end, literally. He stood for a moment, deciding what to do, when a strange idea began to form in his mind. I wonder if I said that word Nan told me, he thought. He said it, "Serendipity!"

He stared at the little door hopefully, half-expecting it to open by itself, but it didn't. "Think, Bentley, think!" he told himself, his eyes moved from the hook to the door and back again. He took a step forward and one of the floor tiles lifted up as his foot caught it, tripping him as he went. That had never happened before, he thought.

He lifted the carpeted tile up and then he saw it. Hidden under it was a chain, curled up in a deep recess in the floor, only it wasn't the floor, it was a trap door. Suddenly, he knew what the door and hook were for. "Ha, that Serendipity thing works! Nan was right!" he whispered. "Let the game be ventured!"

He removed the other carpeted tiles from around the edge of the trap door and lifted out the chain. He pulled on it and the old door creaked on its arthritic hinges, not used in years. As he did so a stale damp smell rose from within. He fastened the chain up onto the hook on the wall, praying that it wouldn't snap after so many years of disuse.

Bentley kneeled to peer down into the dark chasm that stared back at him. A set of stone steps led sharply downwards but he couldn't see a thing. Nervously, he edged his way down into the intimidating hidden cellar. As he descended the first few steps, he fumbled for a light switch, but found none. He made his way back up and found a candle and matches in the drinks cabinet which for some reason his mother had insisted on keeping in the dark corridor. He placed the candle into the top of an empty bottle of 'Navy Strength' Plymouth gin and lit it. Now he was ready to discover what all the mystery was about.

Whatever the spirit from the dead wanted from Bentley, he knew that it was down in the cellar, waiting to be confronted. He only had to go in and hope the door didn't come crashing down and lock him in… perhaps forever.

Outside, in the garden, Sherlock gave a low growl as someone approached the house with dark intentions.

Now armed with the candle, Bentley ducked his head as he descended into the cold, dank cellar. The candle flame shed light onto a place which had remained in darkness for nearly a hundred years.

He stepped tentatively off the last step and brushed aside the cobwebs that clung to his face and clothes. There were two small rooms with white flaky brickwork and shelves that had probably once held provisions for the household. He crossed the flagstones into a smaller more cramped room. In it, in the centre, was a table upon which rested something he had not been expecting. Isn't that a - he thought to himself. I have to speak to Marina.

He stepped closer. It was an intricate and beautiful candelabra. He froze when he saw it and went dizzy. It had some strange effect on him. He staggered back and his mind took him to another place, the shiny silver object stood there alongside other equally precious things gleaming under the electric light. But there was something wrong, something dark despite the sparkling lights. Bentley felt quite sick, his imagination was playing tricks on him. The object had cast a spell over him. What was this?

Then he slumped against the wall, stopping himself from crumbling to the floor. Wiping the cold sweat from his brow, he took deep breaths to beat the nausea rising within him. He straightened up and moved closer to the strange object. Now he saw there was inscription wrapped around its square base:

'A country without land, its kings and dignitaries are lifeless. If the king is annihilated, no one is left alive - 18'

There was that number 18, again! he thought, quite forgetting the haunting hour. But what did it mean? The rest of the riddle seemed obvious enough, but the reappearance of the number baffled him completely. He would definitely have to speak to Marina, she would know for sure, but he didn't think she would know why it had made him feel so dizzy.

He walked back towards the steps and then heard whispering. At first, he couldn't work out the words but then they repeated themselves. Fear rushed through his veins. He was underground. No one knew he was there. If the door came down, or worse still, if something came after him, he couldn't escape. He froze and then he heard the words more clearly.

"Come back, come back," they hissed softly, calling after him. His limbs began to stiffen with fear and he barely managed to shuffle to the steps before he heard the words again. This time they were much louder, and he felt cool air on his ear, *"Come back, come back!"* He struggled to remain calm but when the candle blew out, he bounded up the stone steps with superhuman speed, his limbs discovering miraculous hidden strength at the last moment. Once out of the cellar, he quickly unhooked the chain, trying to block out the words which had grown more urgent, "Come back! Come back!!"

Bentley released the chain and just before the trap door slammed down, he thought he saw the faint outline of a figure coming up the steps.

He had lost his cool. All that effort to then chicken out at the last. He would have to be stronger next time. He would try again, but not just now.

Sweat poured down his back. His lungs heaved with panic. He stepped on the trapdoor to leave the corridor and as he did, something banged against it. Bentley felt the impact on the soles of his feet. It was violent, tripping him up and shaking the whole room. He stumbled, then caught his balance and returned to the living room. When he came out of the narrow corridor, he breathed a huge sigh of relief - the noise had stopped. He knew that it was an empty victory because soon he would have to go back down there.

But just when he thought he had been given a momentary respite there came the sound of scratching. He looked around the room with wild eyes. Then he saw Sherlock locked outside in the cold night, whimpering to be allowed back in. Bentley opened the back door and the dog came running in, his nose low to the ground, his ears alert. Bentley picked him up.

As he did so he noticed wet boot prints leading from the door, to the corridor and then back again. It was clear that someone had entered the house when he had gone into the cellar. And whoever it was had somehow managed to unlock the back door.

"You, Sherlock, are not going anywhere in the house, if it's without me," stated Bentley firmly as he locked the back door. And the pair of them sat down on the sofa to watch TV and wait until Bentley's parents returned home.

When they did come home, Bentley had to find the words to explain the mysterious footprints without it sounding as if he were either mad or making things up. To his surprise his father took him at his word and phoned the police at once.

But despite the intervention of the forces of law and order, Bentley could sense that things were beginning to spiral out of his control.

PART TWO
- SPANISH ARMADA -

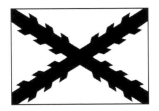

THE ARMADA
1588

Drake boarded the *Revenge* and inspected the two castles, fore and aft. He looked over her side; she sat lower in the water than normal ships and carried 46 guns.

"She's a race-ship, all right," someone said.

"Ah, Moses," replied Drake, "She's a race-ship indeed, and the Spanish will not get close to her or the other 24 we have with us. Hawkins and I designed them well. Her hull is a cod's head and she has a mackerel tail."

"There is not the like on the seven seas, Cap'n."

"Aye, the rules of engagement have changed and today Old Spain is going to see it."

"Captain Drake," came a voice, interrupting the conversation.

"Don Alvaro, our Portuguese ally," acknowledged Drake, "are you ready to take on the Spaniards and take your country back?"

"That I am, Captain, but I must speak with you."

"Speak, man."

"On the poop deck, please."

"You can speak here. Moses will give us the deck."

"Aye, aye, Cap'n," nodded Moses and went below.

"Captain Drake, it is an honour for me to sail with you this day and I will give my life in battle. It is also my sworn duty to defend the captain of this ship."

"You fight for your own soul, and I'll take care of mine."

"But I must insist that your life is in danger with the threat of spies all around."

"If you sees one, you be sure to tell me," said Drake in a jovial spirit.

"I have."

Drake's seemingly mild manner froze, "And where is he, exactly?"

"Below decks - Moses."

"Again with this prejudice of yours!"

"I am serious."

"So am I."

"I remind you, he is a Jew," insisted Mendez.

"My name being questioned?" spoke Moses, appearing on deck.

"Only your faith," replied Drake in annoyance.

"That old story again, is it?"

"His faith is no concern o' mine, and neither is it yours," continued Drake, turning back to face Mendez. "Only his allegiance to me, this ship and England is what counts today and thereafter. Do not undermine me trust in me best man! We do not know each other, Senhor Mendez, but you knows me reputation. We shall exchange no more words on this or you'll be tried for treachery and do the Marshal's dance from that there beam. On board this ship, I am judge and jury."

Alvaro Mendez, frustrated but subdued, bowed and turned to leave. As he went, he brushed past a defiant Moses, who locked eyes with him, but Mendez's gaze was distracted by an object seemingly hidden in the helmsman's tunic. Was it Drake's gold? he thought. He had to find out.

"Is that a weapon you carry, concealed with you?" he asked Moses.

"It's a dagger," answered Moses in a sarcastic tone, "and I'll be stabbing our cap'n here the moment we leave protection of the coast."

He looked at Drake, who burst out laughing, slapping him on the shoulder.

"Don't get flustered there," Moses said calmly to Mendez. "Me cap'n here entrusted a special 'something' to me, and it'll be worth a pretty sum one day. So, no need to be worrin' about safety aboard ship."

Mendez looked offended and stormed off. He would have his revenge and his fortune on this venture, come what may.

"And Senhor Mendez!" Drake called after him, "I am not Cap'n, I'm Vice-Admiral," and stared coldly into his eyes to drive home his displeasure. "You'd be well to remember that."

"Aye, aye... Vice-Admiral," and with that Mendez disappeared below decks as the ship readied to make sail.

Drake looked up to the crow's nest. "What do you see, man?" he yelled up to the top mast. There was no reply as the man jittered about in the heights. Then he pointed out to sea and looked down at his captain. Drake ran to the forecastle of the ship and leaned out to see over the bowsprit. Then he saw it. A black line appeared across the horizon, which gradually grew in stature and sail. He looked across at the other ships of the English line and they had all seen it as men hastened across decks.

The monstrous floating Spanish castles, under which the sea herself was heard to groan, were dressed in a colourful pageant as if honouring the certain victory they believed would soon be theirs by God's right. Then the red flags with their yellow crosses of the Armada came into clear view.

A plume of smoke jettisoned out from one of the grand Spanish galleons. It was followed by a soundless pause until the explosive crack in the air of cannon fire washed across the English fleet. Then the *San Martín* ran up the royal standard.

Drake spied the flag flying proudly on the ship's mast, "Alonso... Pérez... de Guzmán," he whispered, "Duke of Medina Sidonia - our Dutch spies have served us well."

Lord Howard returned the Spanish challenge with a salvo from the *Ark Royal*. They were now at war, and it would not be long before men would be at the bottom of the sea and torn apart on shattered decks.

Drake climbed up the shroud rope ladder, steadying the main mast to get a clearer view of the Spanish movements. He saw the fleet was regrouping in battle array and descended the shroud to join Moses.

"They're in crescent formation," he said to his helmsman.

"The galleasses at the points?"

"Aye, to protect their supply ships in the centre. But while these galleasses have oars and work against the wind, they are a Mediterranean vessel and not made for strong waters such as these."

"Great seamanship that is."

"The best," answered Drake, and then fell silent.

"Why did they not sink us in Plymouth?" asked Moses.

"They seem keener to land their troops from the Netherlands than engage at sea, but they have made their first error. With luck, me dear Moses, there will be more misjudgements. This Duke of Medina Sidonia, who leads this Enterprise of King Felipe, is not a naval man, nor eager for the fight, despite his noble blood."

The prevailing south-west wind blew them north-eastward at a gentle rhythm as the sun began to fall behind the horizon. Both crews had been spared battle on the first day by the Grace of God, but with daybreak, God would not be so generous in offering such grace to all.

- XIX -

NUMEROLOGY
1982

"Morning class," greeted Miss Wheat, but the pupils secretly referred to her as Miss 'Sweet', due to her prim appearance, flawless complexion and bright, starry eyes. All the pupils loved her.

She noted some of them mumbling.

"What is it?" she asked.

"Nothing, Miss," said Tuttle.

"Really?" she replied.

"You know, Miss... it's *Maths* class, isn't it?" said Stanton.

"What? You don't like Maths?!" she said defensively.

"Does anybody?" said Tuttle.

"I do!" piped up Marina.

"And me!" said Wendy.

"Maths is magical," ended Jane.

"Quite," said Miss Wheat, smiling at her supporters.

"How so?" said Bentley.

"I shall now demonstrate by reading your mind."

"Really?" he said.

"Really. Get a pen and a scrap of paper, Bentley. Choose any number between 1 and 20. And just to make it credible, first write it down on a piece of paper and show two or three people nearest you."

"Okay," he scribbled the sum next to his number.

"Now add 5 to it."

He nodded

"Now multiply that total by 3."

"Done."

"Wait, there's more. Now subtract 15 from the result. Miss Wheat waited. "Okay, what's your total?"

"24."

"Right, so that must mean your number is… eight."

Bentley's face collapsed in stunned amazement.

"Wow!" shouted Burt. "It's eight!" he said, snatching the paper from Bentley's hand and holding it up with his finger covering the number everyone wanted to see.

"But Maths is much more than that," continued Miss Wheat. "It is even spiritual, according to the Ancients. There are magical numbers in the Bible such as 3 and 7. For example, how long did it take God to create the Earth?"

"Seven days," said Marina.

"Correct, Hernan. And Jesus asked God 3 times if he could avoid crucifixion and was crucified at 3 in the afternoon."

The class were enthralled.

"On the subject of religion, what is the number of the Beast - the Devil?" she asked, taking their curiosity further.

"666," came an enthusiastic Tuttle.

They all knew about the film *The Omen*. Stanton had even seen it at the cinema and Burt had read the novel. Neither of them slept for a week afterwards.

"So, that begs the question what is the number of the Lord? If the Fallen Angel has a number, then it goes without saying that Jesus should also have one, and he does - it's 888."

"Why 888?" asked Bentley.

"There are different theories for that, but chief among them is numerology, where each letter has a numerical value and that number can be lucky or not, and therefore determine your future - but I think that's balderdash. Anyhow, Jesus in Ancient Greek was *Iesous*, which in turn is the transliteration of the Hebrew *Jeshua,* and each letter adds up to a total of 888."

"Miss Wheat?" called out Bentley, hoping he might learn something, "what about the number 18?"

"You really are getting into this - it's not to keep me from giving you sums to do now in class, is it?"

There was a guilty silence in the room.

"I'm serious," insisted Bentley.

"I can see you are," she said.

"Is there any special meaning for the number 18 in the Bible?"

"I don't know about the Bible, but I do know that it is a lucky number in China, where it is associated with becoming wealthy."

"It's good luck in Hebrew as well," added Marina. "The Hebrew word for 'life' has the numerical value of 18. That's why when Jewish people donate money, they always give money in multiples of 18."

Marina's information got Bentley's imagination firing.

"Well, I never knew that," said Miss Wheat. "Thank you, Miss Hernan. Okay, what I think we will do is reveal the numerical value of each of your names, and that way we can learn whether it is a lucky number or not. Do you want to do that Tuttle or is it too *boring* for you?"

"No, no. Sounds great, Miss!"

The class needed no further persuasion that Maths could be interesting.

"Are you here, Bentley," asked Mrs Wheat, who caught him staring out the window.

"No, I mean yes Miss, I was just thinking about the Twin Tors next week."

"Ah, the dreaded Twin Tors."

The mention of the Twin Tors killed the previous excitement in an instant.

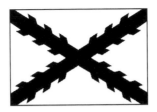

XX

ENGAGEMENT
1588

"Mendez," commanded Drake, as the two men enjoyed a tranquil moment on deck before the rest of the men that were huddled on the open main deck stirred awake, "An assessment of the enemy."

Pipe smoke began to fill the dawn air as voices exchanged early impressions. The 250-man crew prepared the ship for what would come, then Mendez returned to Drake to make his report.

"Very well, Mendez," said Drake on hearing the information, "We shall follow the Armada at this distance until Lord Howard gives the order to engage. For the time being, I wish to know me position, Senhor Mendez."

"Aye, aye, Vice-Admiral."

Moses smiled at Mendez still forcing himself to address Drake as Vice-Admiral, while the rest of the crew referred to him directly as 'Cap'n'. Drake acknowledged Moses' mirth but maintained his stern expression.

As Mendez returned to the main deck, he fixed his stare on Moses' tunic. Moses tapped the slight bulge knowingly. "Who knows?" said the helmsman, "maybe one day I'll have enough money for me own ship and you can be my second-in-command."

The jealousy welled up uncontrollably inside Mendez. He glanced briefly at Moses' tunic again and then fixed Moses' eyes, "We'll see who walks off this ship a rich man," and left wearing a devilish grin, which all nearby saw except Drake.

If Mendez had been watching Moses to protect Drake, he was now more interested to walk away with Moses' prize than hunt down a spy.

It was well into the afternoon when Drake was at last given the signal he had been waiting for: to give fight to the Spanish. The crews spotted people who had come to the coast to witness the fearful scene. A battle upon whose outcome their immediate futures were dependent.

The race-ships under Drake garnered the wind and advanced toward the western fringe of the half-moon formation, where the heavily fortified galleasses were primed for action, their oars ready to be dispatched, should the wind drop. The crescent moon bulged convexly away from the English fleet and eastwards up the Channel, so as to hinder any attempt by the English to attack the defenceless boats concentrated in its centre; lest the English wished to be encircled by Spanish warships.

"Enemy is two points off the starboard bow, Vice-Admiral," communicated Mendez.

"Keep her on this course helmsman, and do not let them come any nearer. We're gaining handsomely. We will use our artillery. They will try to board us, but we shall not let them get close enough. We're too fast and manoeuvrable for them. There'll be nothing they can do."

The balmy air and blue sky would have been a perfect moment to contemplate the beauty of life and one's own existence, but instead the crew could only think of the approaching veil of death and their own mortality, exposed to the threatening waves and muzzles of foreign canon. The air was filled with men shouting and the sound of the wind straining on the sails, as every man's nervous heart was filled with the fear that they were about to engage in war.

Engagement

As Drake's ship, *Revenge,* was reaching its final preparations to open fire, a volley of cannon burst forth, spitting flames and smoke over the water surface. Sir Henry Palmer of *Antelope* had opened fire on one of the Neapolitan galleasses that had turned to engage him. Some moments later and *Antelope* fired off another cannonade, abandoning the scene, to leave the galleass no target to fix its sights upon.

A long silence followed as the giant floating structures, on both sides, lumbered about like arthritic sea creatures, seeking a favourable line of attack. The Spanish ships broke formation on the edges and bobbed around as they turned slowly.

The Spanish vainly tried to bring about a full engagement, and then the ships began to close quarters, making the task of the race-ships more complicated to escape the snares of the giant Spanish galleons.

The fight intensified and an engagement between Jeremy Turner's *Bull* and another galleon saw a latent explosion that filled the battle site with smoke, fire and mortal flying debris. The entire aft section of the Spanish ship blew up into the air, spreading shattered timber in all directions. Mercifully the light began to fade, and the natural harbinger ushered in a cessation of hostilities as had been the plan for the first day of conflict. The English had learned all they needed and regrouped to consider revised battle tactics.

The English would later pick up a Dutchman floating among the wreckage, pleading their help. The man was the master gunner of the *San Juan* and eagerly explained that after an altercation with his captain, the captain had delivered him a full blow to the face with a stick. In a fit of volcanic fury, the master gunner had descended below decks and set a long-lighted linstock to a powder keg, jumping out of a porthole before the ensuing explosion ripped the ship from stern to stern.

When the English crew learned of this incredible feat, the captain told his men to treat the Dutchman kindly, and they took him below and put him under secure lock and guard, far from any source of shot or powder. The English, meanwhile, counted no losses among their ranks or vessels after the first day of fighting.

That evening, Lord Howard called the captains to his ship for a council of war.

XXI

THE TWIN TORS
1982

The eight boys and girls stood in the blustering winds in the aptly-named 'Four Winds' car park with their backpacks at the ready. They huddled around the headmaster with their parents to hear his instructions.

"First up, very well done all of you for braving the elements to participate in our annual Twin Tors challenge - a long-established tradition at Forcastle College and certainly not for the faint-hearted. Today will be especially demanding due to the changeable weather that Dartmoor is famous for. I wish you all the best and hand you over to Mr Pendrift."

"Good morning to you, one and all, on this most splendid of mornings. Mr Troswell's group, which is Hernan, Bentley, Tuttle and Britton, will start off. My group: that is Wilcove, Werrington, Stanton and Burton, will follow an hour later. We start here at Merrivale, pass by Grey Wethers, up to Cranmere Pool and then on to Watern Tor. After a bite to eat we will then head back down to Hound Tor, via Grimspond, before making our way to our pick up point at Haytor.

Bentley caught Marina's attention, "There's something I really need to ask you," he whispered.

"Not now, let's listen."

"It's really important."

"You sound mysterious."

"It is."

Marina raised her brows in surprise, but then turned to hear the rest of the briefing.

"Naturally, each group will navigate their own path, overseen by Mr Troswell and myself. The headmaster will keep time for each group. May the best team win! And we will see each other on the other side of the moor."

There was a brief, if muffled, applause as the small group clapped through their woollen gloves.

"So, Mr Troswell, if your party's ready," piped up the headmaster.

"Three… two… one… go!"

The group stayed motionless.

"Okay, who's got the map?" asked Mr Troswell, turning a deep shade of red, as the unimpressed and cold parents stared at them in disbelief.

"Here, sir," said Marina.

"And I have the compass, sir," said Britton.

They all gathered round to get their bearings, while everyone else waited with frosty boredom.

Soon they got going and headed north, up the small incline and into the great expanse of Dartmoor's Bronze Age wasteland. Gone were the cramped views of inner-city Plymouth and in their place was a forbidding, endless sky. After a brief but brisk five-minute hike they were already feeling the strain. Mr Troswell stopped them at one of the focal points of their trip.

"This is the first point of reference. Take a good look around - we have to spend 10 minutes here before moving on."

"What are these rocks?" asked Britton.

"This is Merrivale's main attraction," answered Mr Troswell. "Here are a group of round houses; two double stone rows and one single row; a small stone circle, with two standing stones over there; as well as a number of earthen mounds, called cairns - something to do with burials."

"So, this is from the Stone Age?" said Bentley.

"Bronze Age," said Mr Troswell. Britton scoffed at Bentley's ignorance.

"Actually, it's both. Neolithic - *New Stone Age*, and Bronze Age, from about 2500 to 1000 BC," added Marina.

"Look who's a know-it-all," jeered Britton.

"I read up on Dartmoor before we came out."

"What? D'you want a star for being able to read?"

"No, but you'd be a star if you disappeared."

"Now then, you two," interrupted Mr Troswell. "There's nothing to stop me from giving either of you a good thrashing if you don't put a lid on it."

Bentley wished he had also done a bit of reading before the challenge.

"And that stone row," she continued, "is the longest of its kind in the world. There are 75 on Dartmoor."

"Wow!" said Bentley and walked off to take a closer look. "How long is it?"

"Over 250 metres."

After everyone had wandered around the site, Mr Troswell called them to a meeting.

"We're now heading for Grey Wethers," he said, "so set your course from here, direction North East."

The wind now came side on as they set out across the empty landscape. The test of endurance against the elements had begun. The hills swayed about like heavy seas, their granite topped Tors, the crests of blackened waves, breaking in the tempest.

"The moor looks like the land that time forgot," said Bentley.

"Move it you two chatterboxes, or you'll get left behind!" called out Mr Troswell and then pointed at the horizon. Grey skies were closing in and falling to earth. "You don't want to get caught in any fog, or the Hound of the Baskervilles will be after you!"

"Is that based on Dartmoor?" asked Bentley. "I thought it was Bodmin Moor."

"That's another beast on Bodmin. But yes, the Hound story is from Dartmoor, all right."

Bentley tried to swallow but his throat had gone inexplicably dry.

As they walked, their feet struck against the tufts of grass that hindered their every step. The wind beat against them with unrelenting force and malice, obliging them to bend their heads and avoid its spiteful attempts to suffocate them. It was clear that Dartmoor didn't want them there. It had spat out Bronze Age man and had equal contempt for its modern descendants.

Their legs soon began to feel like cumbersome sandbags. Up the final slope they went as Mr Troswell, Tuttle and Britton awaited their late arrival.

"Come on!" called out an impatient Britton, "our 15-minute stop can't begin until you get here!"

Marina and Bentley started to run but after just five strides they gave up. They passed Mr Troswell, "Right, 15 minutes from now," he said. "Take a look around the two stone circles and then we'll be on our way."

None of them could move though, and all four of them left Mr Troswell to explore on his own as they propped themselves up against the dry-stone wall to renew their strength. Their faces were red from the effort and chapped from the cold.

"So," said Britton, addressing Marina, "you think you know everything. What's this place then?"

"Get your breath back," said Bentley, "don't bother telling him anything."

Marina took a few gulps of air and lifted the hood on her anorak, "Well, each circle is 33 metres in diameter, there are twenty stones in each—"

"All right, all right, don't bore me with the details."

"You asked," replied Bentley.

"Doesn't mean I want to know."

Marina stood up and walked off, taking Bentley with her to explore the ancient monument.

They both looked out toward the large boundary of the distant Fernworthy forest. Verdant pine trees stood along the edge of the moor, like a long line of advancing soldiers that had halted at the edge of no-man's land.

"So, what was it you wanted to tell me?" asked Marina, breaking their silence.

"I'm not sure how to explain it really, but I need some help."

"What kind?"

"I need you to—"

Then they saw Mr Troswell beckoning them to move on.

Bentley stopped, momentarily rooted to the spot. "Did you hear that?"

"The wind you mean?"

"No, someone calling my name."

"Must have been Troswell."

"Must have been."

"Fifteen minutes is up," said Mr Troswell. "So, no time to lose, if we want to catch the other group. Set your compasses for Cranmere Pool."

They fought with their Ordnance Survey maps and plotted their route. Mr Troswell studied the darkening skies, while Britton did his best to keep Bentley and Marina from seeing the compass.

"Can we see where we're going as well?" asked an annoyed Bentley.

"Don't worry, if you get lost you can get your bearings with that radar of yours," Britton looked at Bentley's pointed tuft of hair.

"Actually," said Marina, "radars aren't pointed."

"Are we done?" asked Mr Troswell, breaking off the budding argument.

"It's that way," said Tuttle. Mr Troswell checked the calculation.

"More like, *that* way," he corrected, "or do you want to take us back? And don't look so crestfallen, you silly boy. It's easy to lose your bearings, even with a compass."

They held up their folded maps and followed their teacher. With every step the sky moved nearer to the moor until the hilltops were wreathed in snowy mist.

"We're veering far too much to the west," warned Mr Troswell. "We don't want to enter the Army's firing range."

Bentley thought it odd that Mr Troswell would have the safety of the students at heart but then he realised the man was only thinking about the possibility of himself being blown up by artillery fire.

Tuttle had his head buried in his map when the inevitable happened and he disappeared, tumbling down a slight incline, screaming as he went. Everyone heard the splash. When the four other members reached him, they found him squirming like a turtle stranded on its back. He was attached to his rucksack, which was immersed in a puddle.

Britton, in an uncharacteristic gesture of charity, held out his hand and helped him up, only to let go just before Tuttle was upright and let him fall back into the water. Britton burst out laughing at his cunning.

"Less of the antics," ordered Mr Troswell. "It's dangerous here."

"He's going to drown in a puddle?!" cried out a disbelieving Britton.

"Worse," interrupted Marina, "he'll drown in the bog."

"Rubbish," huffed Britton.

"There are mires all around," Troswell replied. "The granite keeps the water in, you numbskull. People disappear more often than you might think."

"So, why did you bring us to a bog then, sir?" asked Britton, deflecting his ignorance.

"We've come to see the letterbox," said Marina matter-of-factly.

"I forgot to buy a postcard," said Britton sarcastically.

"Just as well, you've no one to send it to," she retorted.

"There it is," said Bentley, pointing ahead of them and putting an end to the squabble.

Mr Troswell bent down and dragged Tuttle back to his feet, before he joined the others already at the object in question.

Marina opened the door of the squat stone structure, topped by a dark slate mantel. Inside the door panel was the message *'Don't take away the visitor's book stamp or ink pad and spoil it for those who come after.'*

"What's the point of this?" complained Britton.

"It's called fun, Britton," said Mr Troswell, pushing him gruffly to one side. "You may remember it from nursery school."

He handed the box inside to Marina, who opened it and removed the rubber stamp to mark their documents.

"This is the original Dartmoor letterbox," explained Mr Troswell, who seemed happy for the first time. "There are a host of them. Some with secret locations, some containing riddles to the locations of others. It's a culture of its own, conjured up by Dartmoor hikers."

Britton didn't look interested but opened Tuttle's rucksack all the same, so the pair of them could stamp their documents, but all he pulled out were soggy sheets of paper.

"That'll teach you for throwing me back in," said Tuttle scornfully.

Britton threw the paper onto the ground.

"Don't you dare leave anything here!" scolded Troswell. "Pick it up!"

Britton retrieved the offending litter and went to put it back in Tuttle's backpack, but Tuttle dodged and refused to let him do it.

"Put it in your pocket," ordered Troswell. Britton reluctantly did as he was told.

Bentley noted the oddity of the situation: here was Troswell, who didn't care much for the human species, certainly not of the student variety, and yet he seemed to care deeply about the Moor.

Troswell returned the metal container inside the letterbox, and with the formalities completed they could admire the small depression they were standing in. The encroaching mist hung above them and then slowly it began to descend, engulfing them in an eerie white blindness.

"Just up here then," said Troswell, "and we're on our first Tor of the day. Everyone keep close, your eyes on the ground and ahead of you."

No one dared ask exactly how they were supposed to look in two different places at once.

When they reached the mist-covered summit, they almost walked into the impressive columns of layered rocks that stood in scattered piles. They appeared like giant cookie sculptures all stacked up one upon another. The group spent a moment walking round the slabs of ancient exposed granite, dressed in the milky clouds and then rested up.

"Have a bite to eat here," instructed Troswell, "but don't wander off too far."

Bentley and Marina headed to an outcrop of piled up rocks to be by themselves.

"What's this?" asked Bentley.

"A cairn."

"And that is…?"

"Just a pile of rocks to mark a burial site or something symbolic. Dartmoor is full of them."

Bentley bit into his BLT, "I would offer you some, but it's pork and as you're Jewish…"

"I understand," she replied calmly as if hiding something.

"It's strange, don't you think?"

"What is?" she asked.

"God banning pork."

"He can ban what he wants, can't he?"

"There are other meats far dirtier and riskier for your health than pork though. You know, rabbit, chicken. Why didn't he ban one of those?"

"Beats me," she said, bored by the topic.

"I mean, even from a culinary point of view it's weird. Take chicken. It's always chicken. Grill it, fry it, boil it, roast it, it still tastes like chicken and with the same sinewy texture. But pork… that doesn't happen with pork. It's a versatile meat, that's what my father says. So, if God really banned pork then he's no gourmet. That's all I'm saying."

"Fascinating," said Marina, more bored than ever. Bentley got the message and fell silent. "You know," said Marina, breaking the silence, "it's really spooky here in the mist."

"It is, isn't it?"

"Not surprising then that the author Conan Doyle set *The Hound of the Baskervilles* here, is it?"

"Doyle said that the Moor wind sang with the sweet deathly howl of a siren, tempting the naive listener to fall into the trap and forfeit their life."

"Did they really have sirens back in the day of Sherlock Holmes?" asked Bentley innocently, not as well-read as Marina.

"What do you mean?"

"You know, police sirens."

"Not that kind of siren, dummy! A siren is from Greek mythology. Their singing would lure naive sailors onto the rocks and to their deaths."

"Oh, I see."

Bentley wondered if that was what he had heard calling his name before and then a shiver ran down his spine.

"Anyway, tell me more about the help you want from me," she said.

"You're not going to believe this, but I've found a secret basement in my house."

"How old is your house?"

"Over 150 years."

"What did you find down there?"

"A riddle."

"Go on."

"Okay: *'A country without land, its kings and dignitaries are lifeless. If the king is annihilated, no one is left alive - 18'*."

"That's easy enough."

"Seriously?"

"I'm always serious. It refers to chess. I'm not sure about the number 18 though. But how exactly did you discover the basement?" Bentley fell silent.

"I'd rather not say."

"Oh, you have another mystery now. You really are getting my attention."

"If I told you, you'd only laugh."

"Trust me, I'm serious."

"I heard noises."

"What? You mean a ghost?"

Bentley's silence said it all.

"A ghost!" she said in a quiet, mysterious voice, and then burst out laughing.

"You said you were serious," said Bentley, visibly offended.

"Yes, but that's not serious. Honestly, you expect me to believe that a—"

"Why not? This whole moor is full of ghost stories."

"For example?" she asked.

"At Bradford pool people have heard their name called out while they were trapped in the mire; or there's the ghost of

Mr Childe, frozen to death while out hunting and now carried by phantom monks; or the sound of battle at Gidleigh Bridge, where people have also seen the shadow of a woman who drowned there. There is also the ghost of the hanged farmer who took his life after being conned at a fair. He has been seen on his horse making his last journey home. Even there at Cranmere Pool, a former Okehampton mayor is said to haunt the water. I could go on."

"I'm sure you could. Fascinating. Bentley, you really know a lot about ghosts. I thought you said you didn't read much, but they are as you said: stories."

"All the same, I need your help."

"How?"

"Did you hear that?" said Bentley ignoring her last question.

"Apart from the wind? Nothing."

"Exactly - they've gone!"

"What's gone?"

"The others!"

"Impossible! Britton knew where we were."

"That's why we got left behind. I bet Mr Troswell has just walked on like always and not looked back to check. How do we know where to go next?"

"We're going to die from exposure out here, if we get lost."

- XXII -

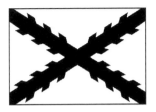

TREASON
1588

The lantern breathed into life as night accompanied the slow fleet up the Channel. In the fading light, one of the watchmen spied something and raced down the shroud from the crow's nest to alert Drake.

"So, you're saying Hawkins has picked up that galleon that blew its aft," answered Drake, "and there's another vessel not far off, also set adrift?"

"She has spent her foremast and bowsprit," said the watchman, "thus being thrown behind her company, Cap'n."

"Position?"

"Three points off the port side."

"Senhor Mendez," said Drake, addressing the man to his right, "douse the lantern."

"But, Vice-Admiral, the fleet is following its light, without it they will be thrown into disarray."

"Are you giving the orders round here now?"

"No, Sir Francis but—"

"They do not need me to guide them up the Channel, and we must lay our hands on that vessel."

"This is no time for piracy. This is a Man o' War, not a venture galley!"

"This is no time for mutinous talk. Carry out your duty as I see fit or I'll be calling the Master at Arms to take you below in chains."

Mendez nodded in obedience and marched to the bow and doused the burning lantern as ordered.

Drake muttered his disagreement to himself, biting his lower lip as he squeezed the hilt of his sword. "Moses - new course. Mark three points to port side."

"Aye, aye, Cap'n."

"Senhor Mendez! Raise all hands! Three points off the port side. You think you can do that now, or will you be needin' a debatin' chamber?"

"No, Vice-Admiral. All hands!" Mendez cried out to the crew and instinctively glanced at Moses' tunic. Good luck charm or not, he wanted it before the fighting was over, then he could lose himself and his new found riches in the chaos and fog of war. "Three points off the port side. Look lively on the halyards."

"Bring up your small arms, Senhor Mendez," ordered Drake. "We're getting ready to ship aboard." Then he turned to Moses, "Lay me alongside at pistol-shot."

The men could see the black bulk of the injured galleon, floating dead in the water, her crew unaware of the approaching English predator. Desperate Spanish voices meanwhile attended the injured and made hasty repairs, but it would be all in vain.

"Stand fast until they're within range," whispered Mendez to the men down on the main deck, their cutlasses in hand and blunderbusses primed to wreak devastation. Just before the two hulls ground together, a few Spanish sailors raised their voices in alarm and tried to find their weapons, but they were too late.

The English screamed as they launched their grappling hooks into the air and fastened them down. The first wave to go aboard stood up on the pinrails and fired their first rounds of shot onto the crowded main deck, spraying a wide arc of destruction across the men. Then the rest of the boarding party jumped over the rails and slashed into the weakened

Spanish. Soldiers were coming up onto deck and a small group had organised themselves on the poop deck, returning fire and felling the first to step aboard. The Englishman manning the small gun aboard *Revenge* spotted the group of resistant soldiers and turned the barrel on them, blowing the top deck to pieces and the men along with it. Soon the English were prevailing on deck and they dispatched wooden grenades down the hatches, hindering any further assistance from the soldiers below.

Mendez and Moses joined the main body of men aboard the Spanish ship. In the chaos of the bloodshed, they ended up side by side. Their blade arms clashed and they both jumped round in a killing-frenzy, preparing to slash the assailant. They recognised each other just as they were about to destroy one another. Their eyes were wild with fire. Then Mendez lunged at Moses and tried to open his tunic. He felt the object.

"A grenade?!" Mendez spat.

"You fool! Have you gone mad?!"

Moses was slow to react, but he removed Mendez's grip and lifted his sword to cut into him but the explosion that came from the deck below threw both men apart. As their eyes opened and they recovered the use of their limbs, they struggled to their feet as Spanish infantry set upon them. Their personal feud set aside.

There followed a final, desperate charge and then the Spanish captain was taken prisoner. With their galleon in ruins and their initial resistance defused, the fight slowly extinguished itself, until the Spanish nobleman called out for the rest of his men to desist, wishing to avoid their futile deaths.

The stricken vessel was towed to Torquay, where the 397 prisoners were kept under guard in the tithe barn of Torre Abbey. Mendez had tried to go with the Spanish ship, loaded as it was with gold coin, but Drake ordered him to stay aboard.

With the Spanish gold coin safely on English shores, Drake lost no further time and set back out to rejoin the English navy.

"Senhor Mendez, bend every sail to catch the fleet."

Drake came aboard *Ark Royal*, where the other captains were already gathered, looking at him as if he had brought the plague with him. Before he had time to address them, Frobisher stormed over and tried to lay his hands on him. Drake, defiant and unrepentant, threw him back. "Get your hands off me, you bilge rat!"

"We should have you strung up for your treason!!"

"Aye!!" called out many of the men lined up behind him.

"You need a mother's hand to guide you through the night now, does ye?!" sneered Drake, staring down any man that dared confront him.

"It was your duty to—" Frobisher tried to continue.

"You don't need me to tell you which way the wind's blowin'. If you can't make way up the Channel, you should not be in command of a fishin' boat, let alone a ship of her Majesty's fleet!!"

"The Spanish could have sunk the fleet because of your actions!! This is treason!"

Lord Howard, watching from the poop deck above, slowly descended the steps to calm the fracas.

Frobisher then addressed the Admiral directly, "Drake's light we looked for, but there was no light to be seen... Like a coward, he kept by the *Rosario* all night because he would have the spoil... We will have our shares, or I will make him spend the best blood in his belly."

"You cheap hypocrite," spat Drake, "you're a gentleman adventurer, as I am, this is your jealous tongue betrayin' ye now. I have not as much as seen a cannon shot in anger from your *Triumph* and ye dare question me actions? Are you a coward now?"

Frobisher moved to draw his sword, but Moses drew his flintlock first.

Lord Howard stepped into the void between the two raging men. "Gentlemen!" he beseeched them. "Sheath your sword and holster your pistol or I'll have both of you doing the gallows dance."

The men calmed their breathing, their eyes still red with ire.

"Drake," continued Howard, "explain your breaking ranks."

"He went after his spoils and left us to the elements," answered Frobisher, heating himself up again.

"Elements you seem ill-prepared to deal with," reposted Drake. "I went after *El Rosario*, the Armada's payship."

"And what was the payoff?" added Frobisher.

"50,000 ducats."

"Ha!" mocked Frobisher. "Only thinkin' of his purse!"

"I was not to know that, when I went after her."

"You are nothin' but the 'supplementary navy', as they say," added Frobisher.

"From their captain I have learned that their cannon are not well provisioned with shot, carry the wrong calibre and can only fire once in the fight."

"And what does that tell us?" scorned Frobisher.

"That we can get closer to drive home our artillery."

There was silence. Drake had carried the day, leaving Frobisher alone in his outburst.

"I am satisfied with the information," declared Lord Howard. "You are indeed a fortunate man though Drake, for had the wind changed and the Spanish turned to engage us, I would have seen you hanged before going down with my crew and ship."

"You should hang him all the same," hissed Frobisher.

"A little more fightin'," laughed Drake, "and a lot less yappin', would make you a better man and at the very least a patriot."

"This matter is sealed, gentlemen," said Lord Howard. "Are we agreed?"

Everyone nodded, except Frobisher.

XXIII

LEFT TO DIE
1982

"We're not gonna die," said Marina, "if we stay focused, and think our way out of here."

"What do you mean 'think our way out of here?' Are we supposed to close our eyes, click our heels and chant 'take me home, take me home?' "

Marina didn't look impressed, "Have you got the compass?" she asked, completely ignoring Bentley's previous outburst.

"Britton's got it."

"Of course."

"Now what?"

"Have you got a watch?"

"Yep."

"Great! We're saved," said a relieved Marina. "All we need to do is point the minute hand at the sun and then draw a line through the central point between the two hands. That line will point north."

"But it's overcast," said Bentley.

"I know, but now and again there is a slight break in the clouds and we can see which direction the sun is coming from. We don't need a perfectly clear day for this to work."

"Okay," Bentley took off his watch and gave it to Marina.

"Have you gone barmy?!" she cried.

"No."

"This is a digital watch, Einstein! Tell me how, exactly, am I supposed to point this at the sun and find north?"

"Erm… I hadn't thought of that."

"And don't suggest a sundial, please."

Bentley looked pensive for a moment. "That's it! Genius! Marina, we don't need watch hands, you're right. All we need to know is the correct time and we have that: it's ten thirty. Now it's just a case of making an outline of the time on the ground, by using two pens, for example."

Bentley rummaged around and found a pen and a pocketknife. Marina jolted with slight alarm as Bentley unfolded the knife.

"Don't worry," he said, "it's just for protection."

"From what?"

"The pixies of course."

"The what?"

"You know, the little people who inhabit the barrows and dolmens, they come out at night to dance around the stone circles."

"No, I don't know."

"Really?" Bentley was stunned.

"Well, that must be just one of the differences between you and me."

"What? That I know the fun stuff and you know the boring stuff?"

"I know the relevant things and you remember what is useless, more like."

"That is another way of looking at it, I suppose." They both laughed.

"Anyway," said Bentley, "the sun seems to be coming from over there, so I point the hour hand, that's the pen in this case, at it. This here," he pointed at a position on the ground, "would be twelve, here three, six and nine. So, ten would be about here and half past ten, with the penknife, would be like so."

"Meaning," finished Marina, as she looked for the direction of the sun, "if we draw a line through the hour and minute hand, the line down the middle of the angle would point south, meaning north is in the opposite direction."

"Exactly!"

They were ecstatic with their calculation and shook hands, as they set off triumphantly.

Bentley and Marina came down from the wind-swept Tor to be met by the rain that had been threatening all morning. They pulled up their anorak hoods as the pitter-patter on their jackets began to increase in volume. Then they heard running water.

"Look," said Marina. "There's a clapper bridge. What a stroke of luck."

"That water looks as dirty as tea."

"Peat soil."

They trudged on, the rainwater now seeping through their trousers. The sensation of cold on their faces and hands worsened. Yearnings for home and the warmth of a log fire began to grow.

A group of Dartmoor ponies, grouped tightly together for protection from the elements, nodded as the two trekkers passed them by.

"What's that?" said Marina.

"A stream. We can cross up there. It's narrow enough for us to leap the gap."

"Hang on a minute," said a suspicious Marina. "Give me the map." She scanned it to check something. "It's Walla Brook, I think."

"How's that possible?"

"That's because we're not where we think we are. Did either of us check to set off south?"

"Oh my God!"

"Exactly," said Marina. "We were so excited to have found north that we just walked off in this direction. So we crossed the river Teign back there. When you said we could *jump* the gap, that sounded the alarm bells."

"Really?"

"Exactly. You can leap a brook, ford a stream and swim across a river."

"Then we're going to have to cross it again," said Bentley.

They turned around and soon found the familiar clapper bridge. Once across it though, the rain sped up and began to fall in scornful lashes.

"We don't have much of an option," said Marina, having to raise her voice over the relentless and deafening rain, "we should get to those trees for some shelter until the rain passes."

Bentley just nodded and the two of them moved as quickly as their sore legs would carry them to the rare sight of trees on the moor and what looked like three walled fields, abandoned long ago.

They marched up a sodden path and through an open stone gateway and discovered what had once been a thoroughfare for a busy farm. The few trees that occupied the lonely ruin alleviated some of the painful rain.

"Here," said Marina, pointing off to the right, "we can shelter under that doorway."

"It's going to be a tight squeeze."

"It's that, or just get pummelled out in the open by this brutal downpour."

They carried on through the gate toward the scattered ruins and the only surviving wall of any significance.

Then Marina screamed and Bentley followed her reaction.

Three sheep rushed out from the ruined building, equally as scared by Bentley and Marina's unexpected outburst.

"For a minute I thought you'd seen a ghost," said a relieved Bentley.

"I told you, they don't exist."

"Yeah, but sheep definitely terrify you!" They both giggled and then their teeth chattered as the cold gripped them again.

"I didn't know they were sheep," said Marina.

"What else around here is dressed in wool, chews grass and bleats?"

"Very funny. Come on, I just want to get under cover."

"Well, you certainly did a cracking job in clearing out the sheep."

They sat down in the doorway, trying to get as comfortable as they could on the cold ground, while water ran past their feet and gales battered against the stonework.

"Do you think this piece we're sitting in here was the farmhouse?" asked Bentley.

"Must have been where they kept the livestock, it's too low for a front door."

"I love ruins," he said.

"Really?"

"They speak of the past. Someone else's life and fate."

"I had never thought of it that way."

"Did you know that Scorhill," said Bentley, thinking of something to take their minds off their dangerous predicament, "just north of here, is the largest stone circle on Dartmoor? The story goes that 'sinful' women would pray for forgiveness at the foot of the stones and if God chose not to be lenient, a stone would fall down on them... Seven of the thirty stones have fallen, but no one knows if any bodies lay underneath."

"That's quite some fairy-tale, but you haven't finished *your* story. Why is it, exactly, you need me to come along to the basement? Moral support?"

"Advice."

"What sort of advice?"

"This," he said, and pulled out a picture.

"It's a mirror."

"And in the reflection?"

"A Star of David, is it? I can't really tell."

"Yes, but how did it get there?"

"It has to be the refracted light from the flash."

"I didn't use a flash. You can see from my reflection here. The camera has no flash."

"Just because I don't have a scientific explanation to hand right at this moment, doesn't mean that there isn't a logical origin for this."

"Isn't it obvious that the *spirit* has done this?"

"If that is the case, and I am very doubtful of such things as you know, then this star can only mean one thing."

"What's that?"

"The spirit, as you put it, is trying to contact you."

"And what is it saying?"

"*I'm Jewish.*"

Bentley fell silent, he didn't get the joke. He just stared at her.

"Now what?" he said.

"Hey! Don't drag me into this!"

"I don't know where to look next."

"You want to follow this thing up? Personally, I'd move house. Who knows? Maybe the ghost wants to you to leave."

"Or lead me to something."

"If that's the case, then perhaps it will go a step further next time. Just don't invite me round."

Then Marina took out her sandwich.

"That was the type of bread that the ghost made!"

"*Shabbat challah.* I remember you had it at school that time," said Marina. "Mrs Nathan, a Jewish family friend, makes it for us now and again. If your ghost exists, then it's *definitely* Jewish. You're serious about this, I see it in your eyes."

"Will you come with me?"

"What? To your house to see this spectre of yours? Absolutely not! Whatever it is, it's calling *you* not me. And there's no guarantee it's not dangerous."

"But what does it want from me?"

"Those that believe in such things say that what all good spirits desire *is…*"

There was a silence as Bentley was expected to finish the sentence.

"A bed sheet?" he eventually answered.

"No! Closure."

"Close what?"

"It means to close the past. Things have been left undone and the spirit cannot rest and move on until its material business in this world has been completed."

"What sort of business?"

"That's for you to find out. You'll have to go back and confront it. My presence would just scare it off."

"Sounds like you believe me."

"No, I'm just being polite."

Bentley pulled out some Kendal Mint cake, seeing the conversation had reached its natural end. Marina twisted open her flask and poured them a drink.

"Tea and biscuits?" she asked brightly.

"Music to my ears."

She handed him a biscuit, and then Bentley felt something brushing against his shoulder. It bleated. The sheep were back and sharing their vital space. He passed the dripping animal a biscuit and then began the wettest and dreariest meal of his life. Bentley and Marina huddled together to conserve warmth in readiness for the long hard walk ahead, social niceties were dispensed with – personal space was a dangerous extravagance.

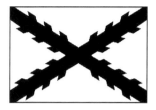

XXIV

THE ENTERPRISE
1588

English merchant vessels marked an unbroken chain from coast to fleet, like marching ants at work, supplying the navy. The local towns, ports and sailors did a brisk trade and it seemed for a moment that war was a welcome business.

When the English finally took to cross the few nautical miles separating England and France, they found the Spanish at length, nestled off the Calais coast, where they were open to the Channel currents, northern elements and English attack.

The English fleet anchored nearby in full view of their prey, firing a salvo to unsettle their foe. Soon they were joined by more ships and now outnumbered the Armada.

Howard called his captains to council.

The men assembled up on the poop deck in their sullied uniforms, unchanged since the first day of campaign, smeared with grease and the stains of toil in battle. Their faces bore the stress of the fight and all signs of humanity had been drained from their hardened eyes. They would kill or be killed.

"The Spanish seem to have made the rash error we have been waiting for," began Drake. "They are too close to the sandbanks and have nowhere to flee."

"We cannot sail into the midst of them, Lord Howard," said an alarmed Palmer.

"There is no need to," spoke up William Wynter, who had joined them from the Dutch coast, "we will employ a well-worn tactic, that even Sir Francis here has used but of late, namely brulots."

"Fireships!" exclaimed Drake.

Palmer nodded in agreement.

"We will wait for nightfall," said Wynter, "and set eight hellburners into their midst."

"And then what?" asked Hawkins.

"We will take advantage of the panic to fire upon them and flush them out into the North Sea or onto the sandbanks nearby," answered Wynter. "They will not be able to get back into the Channel, as we will stay upon their heels and keels."

The council sagely nodded their collective acceptance. They knew how much depended on the ploy. If it did not work, then all could be lost.

The men returned to their command posts as Lord Howard collected up his worst ships for the attack. The *Bark Talbot, Hope, Thomas, Bark Bond, Bear Yonge, Elizabeth, Cure's Ship* and *Angel* were besmeared with wild-fire, pitch, brimstone, gunpowder, rosin and all manner of combustible materials. They prepared each ship away from prying Spanish eyes and then waited for the midnight hour to come.

Meanwhile, Mendez too was building his own plan. He would also take advantage of the darkness, while Moses would have his guard down and no one would be able to come to his assistance.

- XXV -

DARKMOOR
1982

"Where are we exactly?" asked Bentley.

Marina pulled out the map and passed her finger over the relief, "I'd say it would have to be here, Teignhead farm."

"And where next?"

"Well, Grimspound must be in that direction, and it's exactly half-way between here and our final destination at Haytor. But we have to wait out this foul Atlantic weather."

Bentley shuffled his position and something caught his eye. "What's this?" he asked in amazement and pointed at something wedged into a nook in the thick stone door frame. Marina leaned over and pulled it out.

"It looks like we've stumbled upon a secret document for people who are into letterboxing to discover."

"But there's no stamp."

"See if it's still in there."

Bentley poked his fingers into the cranny and pulled out a thin grubby tin box and a tiny rubber stamp. Marina unravelled the rolled-up tube to reveal a sheet of laminated paper.

"How are you supposed to write anything on that?" asked Bentley. "Where's the visitor's book?"

"There isn't one. Not all letterboxes are the same and this one is very different," said Marina, as she scanned the document. Then she smiled.

"What? What is it?"
"It's a poem."
"Really? What's the title?"
"*Darkmoor.*"
"I like it. Go on then, read it out."
"Okay."

Darkmoor...

It is a ghastly, ghostly, godless place
With pagan rites
And Bronze Age sites.
It is a muddy, ruddy, boggy place
Bloodied by time
And dirtied by mines.
Many have come here
And lost their life dear
Swallowed by the mire
Or the wind's harsh ire.

Then the brooding sky lifts
And the sun brings bliss.
Now transformed, it is a different place
Of elegant hills and earthly grace.
Ponies frolic and pixies dance,
Sheep graze, hikers take their chance.
At last it seems that nature can flourish,
In a soulless land unable to nourish.

But the weather closes in and the heavens come asunder
Paradise is lost and emotions grow sombre.
Dartmoor cannot forgive, her denuded state,
Her trees taken from her - man sealed her fate.
Old Father time this mystic granite mound,
Cursing man's kin with the Baskerville hound.

Iron Age forts stand broken all around,
And medieval forests still cling to the ground.
Abandoned farms and ruined villages,
Tell many a tale of haunted vestiges.
Cairn stone markers immortalise great men,
Dry stone circles reveal their Bronze Age dens.

With her peaty rivers and peaky Tors,
Her boundless horizon; she's the paragon of moors."

"Who wrote it?" asked Bentley

"Anon."

"He's written a load of stuff."

"Actually, it's a she," said Marina, and pressed the stamp on the back of his hand, revealing the small green image of the park's iconic pony and the word 'Darkmoor' encircling it. Bentley took the stamp and returned the favour. The document was rolled back up and replaced in the crevice.

"Well, the weather seems to be letting up, so what's at Grimsp—?" Bentley suddenly went silent.

"You'll see. We've got a long hike still ahead of us."

"Did you hear that?"

"What?"

"Someone calling my name again."

"Come on, I'm not falling for that. You'll have to do better!"

"No, I'm serious."

"Let's get a move on, shall we," Marina stood up, packed her flask in her backpack and set off, not waiting to see if Bentley was following. He looked annoyed but followed quickly, the rain had now softened, but they were still at the mercy of an immense overcast sky. Hanging threads of black-grey rain clouds swept over the hills, like giant tendrils, lashing out across the landscape, on their way somewhere down on the coast. Then he felt the presence of someone or something near them.

"Marina!" called out Bentley.

"Hurry up!" she barked back, not bothering to turn round. And then suddenly she disappeared.

"Oh my God!" gasped Bentley, realising what had happened. He threw off his backpack and raced to her through the thick mist that had descended. Her life depended on it. He found her knee deep in a peat bog, gradually sinking into the jaws of the dark chthonic depths. She was twisting and turning to try and free herself, but resistance was useless. In truth, it was deadly.

"Bentley, Bentley!" she cried out. She was sinking so fast there hadn't even been time to laugh at the silliness of it, things had turned serious in an instant.

"Keep still! Keep still!" but she couldn't keep still and sank deeper until the mire was pressing against her lungs. The effort soon sapped her energy, draining her initial outburst and panic attack. She began to hyperventilate.

Bentley knelt at the edge of the peat ring and tried to take her hand, but she had waded in too far.

"Listen," he said, "you have to stay calm or you'll be sucked deeper down. You can get out of this! Trust me!"

Her eyes tightened and tears began to fill them, she was trembling and gasping for breath.

"You have to lie back and spread your limbs out. Then you're going to pull your legs out inch by inch."

She shook her head, helpless at the prospect, "I can't."

"Do it! You must! I'm not going anywhere, there is no rush," he spoke calmly and softly. "Lay back slowly, spread your arms. You won't sink. You have to trust me. Then we'll do your legs."

She huffed several times, taking in air to calm and prepare herself. Then she leaned back, spreading her arms out. Her hair dipped into the murky mix and her hips slowly lifted out.

"That's good. Now rest a moment, and when you're ready, try moving one leg up."

She tried to control her breathing again and pulled on her right leg.

"Okay, rest again. Then we'll try the other in a moment. You're doing great."

And so they went on leg by leg and inch by inch of painstaking work, until mercifully both her feet emerged at the surface. Marina gave a small whimper of joy but then her crying started.

"Okay, stop the crying Marina!" he snapped at her. "We only have time to get serious here."

She looked at him and stopped sobbing at once.

"Now that I know you're listening, you have to roll over towards me, again - slowly, and then I've got you."

Bentley measured up the distance between Marina and his outstretched hand and realised he couldn't reach.

"Ahm… wait here," and he sped off into the mist, "I'll be back with a stick!" he said as his voice trailed off.

Marina twisted slightly, edging her body toward the rim of the bog and nearer salvation. In her feverish haste she moved too quickly and started to sink. Panic seized her as she sensed Death coming to claim her. In a crazed last effort, she flipped herself over and began to sink at an alarming rate, but the extra centimetres allowed Bentley to get a hold on her wrist with one hand. His hand was cold, almost freezing, but she couldn't care less, he had a grip and that was all that mattered. He heaved with all his strength to bring her to safety. Her muddied face fell exhausted on the wet moorland, her legs still half-immersed in the peat bog, but she was alive. She looked up and saw Bentley come crashing through the ferns. Marina was confused.

"You made it!" he said in utter surprise, "how on earth did you do that?"

"You pulled me out?"

"No, I didn't."

"But I felt your hand."

Bentley crouched down and as he did, Marina saw the dark grey figure of a girl standing behind him. She screamed. Bentley turned round in shock, but all he saw was a vacant space and the outline of something disappearing in the mist.

"Help him," heaved a voice on the wind, "help him!" and then it was gone.

Marina had her mouth agape, "Did you hear that?" A shiver ran down her back.

"No," he replied, but he was lying. "It must have been a passer-by." Was something communicating with him? he asked himself. If so, what on earth did it mean?

Bentley pushed his thoughts aside and turned to attend to Marina. She was shivering and soaked. He quickly removed his coat and wrapped it round her, then pulled her legs out of the mire, and cleaned the mud from her clothes and backpack with his towel. Next, he removed her boots, pouring the water out of them. Then he took off her socks, wrung them dry, and fetched the spare pair from her rucksack, rolling them onto her damp feet. After that, he laid down beside her to warm her and wait for her to recover. He noticed that he was also shaking, not so much from the cold, but from the realization that things could have turned out very different."

After a while she smiled weakly at Bentley, "We're going to have to ge-get g-going soon," she jittered, "or the n-night will be upon us if we're n-not ca-careful." Bentley rubbed her shoulders to get more warmth into her limbs. She pulled off his coat, "Th-thanks for that." She hopped slightly to readjust her backpack and took a few limp steps forward. "Come on then Bentley, let's get this over wi-with. I can't be out on the Moor mu-much longer, I'll get hypothermia."

"Right," he replied, giving her a warm smile.

"Bentley," she said and threw her arms around him. "Thanks for being here," Marina was almost crying and snivelling with emotion

"That's what friends are for, aren't they?" Bentley hugged her back. Then he put his arm around her to steady her as they both moved on.

The two lonely figures moved across the vacant landscape, brushed by the winds and harried by the cold. The black sky gave way to a grey patch and a few brave rays of sunshine penetrated the hanging barrier, lighting up a ruined site in the distance.

"Look, Bentley, you can see it from here."

"Grimspound. It's huge." The sighting of the halfway marker gave them a much-needed lift. The undulating black hilltops ran away from them into the horizon, pulling them magnetically along. The large stone circle clung onto the copper-toned hillside, signalling them to come in. They wheezed the last few steps up the slope and passed through the crumbled remains of the ancient settlement's stone entrance. But they hadn't come to look around, just rest and shelter themselves from the wind. Marina pulled out her flask.

"Tea, Bentley? It'll warm you up."

"No, I'm fine," but he wasn't, "you drink up, you need it."

They took their time to get their breath back, and gaze upon the empty Bronze age enclosure.

"Sky's still dark," said Bentley, breaking their meditation. "Not sure if it's overcast or night is setting in."

"Both. We should get going."

"Do you think they'll send out a search party?"

"Depends if Troswell has noticed, but no need, we're almost home."

"Hound Tor next?"

"And it's just up there."

Bentley swivelled round and there, on the summit right above them, was a large outcrop of boulder-like rocks.

"That'll take five minutes," he said.

"And then it's another 3 miles, which is about an hour and a half walk to end at Haytor."

It was an easy climb to the top of the exposed rock that had looked down on them like a formidable fortress. On the other side they saw the familiar sight of a boundless sky, braced by free-ranging winds.

"This is the very tor that inspired the Hound of the Baskervilles," said Bentley, proud of his knowledge and hoping it was something Marina didn't know.

"Really? It does have something spectral about it, you could say."

"Yes, and it's called Hound Tor because a vengeful witch turned some dogs to stone."

"I see the connection now. I didn't know you had read the novel."

"I haven't," Bentley deflated in an instance. "I've only read the comic."

"Something is better than nothing. Come on, no time to lose. That's Haytor there on the horizon."

"You could almost touch it."

"This is the final stretch, Bentley, but first, our next stop is just down there."

They carried on weary and pining for warmth. Marina's boots squelched despite the change of socks and her trousers were stuck to her, cold against the chilling wind. They descended Hound Tor Down and into the valley. Fields and trees came into view, marking the edge of the moor. The vegetation thickened with bracken, gnarled bushes and lilac heather. At last the barren landscape was giving over to some semblance of life. They smiled at each other; home was not far off now.

"Is that another ruin up ahead?" asked Bentley.

"It's the ruined medieval village of Hound Tor. It means we're still on track."

They ambled through the mild grass-covered collection of village ruins and then carried on their way.

"Now, east," said Marina in that confident voice of hers. "There should be a clapper bridge and then we head south for about half an hour, where we should find the remains of an old granite tramway."

"Trams?"

"They carried the stone from the quarry."

As they trudged on, the sound of the odd car passing in the distance met their ears, the first sign of civilisation. They had almost forgotten what it sounded like. They soon found the road and crossed its oil-black tarmac and bright white lines, stepping from the past back into the present. A stray cow was the only one making any use of the well-laid asphalt.

Haytor was right in front of them now and Bentley pointed at the group of people gathered there in all colours of anorak, seemingly looking in their direction.

"I can hear voices," he said.

"Not again."

"Where the devil have you two been!" shouted someone. It was Mr Troswell. Britton and another man were also arriving.

"We got left behind," explained Bentley.

"That's no excuse!"

"It's *every* excuse," remonstrated Marina. Then she saw someone she recognised behind him.

"I didn't ask for your opinion," carried on Troswell. "Your stupidity has caused chaos for the rest of the group! I'll see to it you're both expelled!"

"You should have sent someone to find us," insisted Marina.

"I sent Britton."

"He never said anything to us."

"Yes, I did," chipped in Britton, newly arrived.

"You're lying!" shouted Bentley.

"No, you're the liar!"

"Bentley! Shut it or I'll discipline you here and now if I have to," said Troswell on the verge of losing control.

"Try it!" Bentley said defiantly.

"What did you say?!" Troswell was changing colour.

"You tried to kill us!" Marina shouted at Britton.

Troswell grabbed her by the arm, "Don't you start with that attitude Marina Hernan. Who do you think you are?!!"

"She's my daughter!" bellowed a voice from behind Troswell, pushing him almost into the bracken as the man took hold of Marina, who was on the point of collapse. "And I'll see to it that you are fired for neglect! You should have noticed well before arriving at Haytor and gone back yourself, rather than just sit on your hands waiting for them to find their own way. This is scandalous! Where's your sense of honour, man?!"

Marina's father barged past and went back to join the others. Bentley walked after them, leaving Troswell to contemplate the empty moor, which was exactly how he looked, in his pale shade of shock.

From the high point at Haytor, everyone rushed down to greet them. The headmaster looked almost as relieved as Marina's mother.

Bentley looked for his mother and saw the green Land Rover. Inside his mother was reading the paper. He walked over and knocked on the door.

She wound down the window, "Ah, there you are dear. Have a nice time?"

"We got lost."

"That figures," she chuckled.

"We almost died."

"Well, you look quite alive to me and that's the main thing."

"Marina fell in a bog and nearly drowned."

"Oh, don't be so melodramatic, it was just a walk in the woods."

"Mother, there are no woods out on the moor. That's why it's called Dartmoor and not Dart Forest."

"Stop splitting hairs, you know what I mean. Now, shall we be getting along?"

"I'll just go and say goodbye."

Bentley walked round the back of the vehicle and dumped his rucksack inside. When he returned to the others, he took a detour and walked around the main rock outcrop to give Marina's parents some space to compose themselves, and Marina time to warm up a little. He looked up at the bulbous rock, rising 70 metres above. For a moment his mind was blank, but something stirred him. He turned round, there was nothing there. He walked around the base of the rocks which were covered in lichens and moss. Something seemed to be pulling him to the rock stacks at the far end.

"*Bentley,*" a voice whispered and then it was lost on the wind. His eyes shot open. He walked faster to catch the sound. "*Bentley,*" hissed the voice again. It sounded like a young girl. Was that right?

Then he stopped by a crack in the rock face. The voice seemed to be coming from inside it. He peered into the narrow gap. "*Save him.*" Bentley was immobile. "*Save him for me.*" Then a hand from inside the rock shot out and touched his face. He should have jumped back but instead he allowed the hand to gently stroke his face and then it was gone – evaporated into the air. Who did he have to save?

"There you are, Bentley," said Marina, walking toward him and looking a little better than before. "Are you all right?" Then she giggled.

"What is it?"

"It looks like you just saw a ghost," she laughed.

"Ah," and Bentley blushed, not knowing what to say.

"We looked all over for you. We're going now but I wanted to say something about earlier."

"Oh, don't mention it. You would have done the same had it been me in that bog."

"Not, that, but thanks again anyway. No, I wanted to say, you know about going into the basement in your house. It sounds scary."

"It is."

"Sounds mysterious… and even dangerous."

"Could be."

"Good. Count me in. Just don't say you can hear voices - you're starting to get creepy. Okay?"

"Okay, but you'll *really* come?"

"Of course."

"I thought you said you didn't believe in ghosts?"

"I don't. The only thing I fear is fear itself."

"So, what is your biggest fear?

"What everyone is terrified of the most."

"And what's that?"

"Other people."

"What about spiders?"

"There aren't spiders down there, are there?" she said, alarmed for the first time.

"Just kidding," he answered. Marina relaxed.

"Ghosts I can handle, but spiders… they're real."

She leaned forward and pecked him on the cheek, "That was for saving my life." And then she was gone.

"It was worth it," he whispered after her.

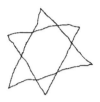

IT
1982

"Right son," said Bentley's father, "you're the man of the house today." Bentley switched off the cricket on TV. "We'll see you later this evening. Don't forget that it's your turn to mow the lawn and when you've finished that then make good use of your time for some serious study. Don't get distracted by the Test Match. You can watch the highlights later."

"And even that's not worth watching," said his mother, fixing her hair in the hallway mirror. "Aagh!!" she screamed. Everyone jumped.

"What's the matter?" asked her husband, who quickly came to the hallway.

"I-I don't know. I-I thought I saw something in the mirror." She was shaking and quite pale, Bentley quickly joined them.

"Come on, dear. It's just your imagination playing tricks on you. It was probably a shadow of a car passing outside," he reassured her.

"Ye-yes, that's what it was. I saw a passing shadow, so it must have been a car as you say."

"Let's get going then, shall we? Oh, and don't worry about any intruders, the police are still keeping a look out."

He scooped up the keys for the Jag, "Remember what I said, lad. You've important exams coming up, if you want to enter Plymouth College."

147

"Yes, Father."

"That's my boy."

The front door closed with a heavy clunk, the car engine grumbled and then once again Bentley was alone. He expected Sherlock to come running out at any second, but he suddenly remembered that he was with his nan. So, he really was alone. The silence seemed to resonate down the passageway and out to the far end of the cottage annex. He would mow the lawn straight away, at least it was a beautiful sunny day.

He hurried outside, checking around him in case someone was lurking in the bushes, and entered the garage. The musky smell of wood and gardening equipment mixed with the pungent smell of oil fumes and the heady odour of car leather seats on his father's classic Austin Healey that occupied the centre of the garage. He dragged the heavy push mower out and onto the grass. As he set about recreating the finest Wimbledon striped lawn in the family back garden, Bentley's mind turned to recent events and the various clues he had amassed.

Nan said something was trying to contact me, but what? he thought. She said I had a gift but I'm not sure what that is either. But something strange did happen when I said that even stranger word 'seren— what was it again? 'Serendipity'. Is that my special talent? It couldn't be, could it? It didn't make sense. But then how did she know about the jeweller? That had happened when they lived in Plympton. And then there was Marina saying that this presence in my house was Jewish. Why was that relevant? But it was definitely odd seeing the seven candles, the number 18 and the interlaced bread, not to mention the Star of David. That was all real. I know it was. And then I saw something disappear down into the basement, didn't I? Or was that my imagination acting like mother's just a moment ago? I could just be going mad - nothing serious. I mean the voice on the moor, what had that to do with any of this? No, it had to be madness. That was good though, better than bumping into a real live... actually... dead, ghost, wasn't it? But whatever it is that is making noises in the house I have to find it and get some answers. If not, I won't be able to get any rest.

By the time he had come to the end of his mowing and mental meanderings, he stopped and looked up to admire his work. The lawn looked ready to host Wimbledon's finest players.

Determined to delay his studying, he returned inside and decided to give the dining room carpet a quick hoover.

He was just passing the vacuum cleaner by the dining table when he remembered that this was the very spot where his nan had said she had felt the presence. It had been during the day as well, he thought, I remember that clearly, and the dog was out, which was a weird detail. Fortunately, Sherlock is here with me. He then remembered again that his faithful companion was at his nan's, and a brief shiver of fear shot down his spine. He smiled nervously to himself. Don't be stupid, he thought, but then his expression froze.

He couldn't explain it, but he just knew it. He could sense that someone, or something, was behind him. It's watching me! he thought. From the hall. It's just as Nan said. Maybe nothing's there. No! There is something there! He almost stopped breathing. Why should I turn round, if I don't want to? Once I see it there's no undoing that image. His thoughts were turning to panic. You'll have it forever Bentley. There'll be no erasing it. Maybe it'll just go away. No one will believe you if you look. But something, inexplicably, was pulling him round to confront it, despite his terror and resistance.

He turned involuntarily. He felt dizzy and his body was trembling with cold fear. Then his vision went blurry as his eyes fell upon a silver-grey, translucent figure. Bentley sucked in his breath, too scared to scream or move. His mind was numb. His thoughts didn't dare speak to him. He just stared and stared, rooted to the spot. The figure meanwhile stood there peacefully. Nothing happened for an eternal minute. Slowly, Bentley became more accepting of what he could see as it meant him no harm, despite the pure adrenalin coursing through his veins. It's a gent, he thought, an elegant gent wearing a morning suit. Bentley then noticed him fidgeting with his watch chain and stroking his beard. Just as Bentley felt the first tingling of calm returning, the figure slowly evaporated, and the moment was over.

He slumped down on a chair until his breathing slowed. He was trembling and light-headed. He was worried he might faint. He walked unsteadily to the kitchen and splashed a glass of water onto his face. He refilled it and leaned into the sink, this time pouring the second glass over the back of his head and neck. The water soaked his shirt, front and back but he didn't notice and didn't care.

I never want to do that again, he thought and then felt a tap on his shoulder. He jumped round screaming at the top of his voice, falling back against the kitchen sink as he pathetically tried to defend himself against an assailant, but it was his father.

"Calm down, son! No need to jump out of your skin. We came back early that's all. The event was called off. No idea why.

"Only in England can something be called off when there's good weather," chipped in his mother.

"But it looks like you've been quite busy," said his father. "Now, off you go and get some study done."

Bentley left as instructed, but there was no settling his mind on academic work. What he had just seen had once again made him ask the question, "Was there really life after death?" He didn't know what else he could make of it; all he knew now was that his next destination was going to be a visit down into the cellar. At least Marina said she would accompany him, but there was no way he was telling her he had actually seen the ghost now. Not because she would think he was mad, but because she may decide to let him go down there alone.

- XXVII -

ROUGH JUSTICE
1982

The summer sunshine was at its best, and the students were in short sleeves as they walked toward the school. Bentley looked to the distant moorland hills, well-rounded like the haunches of a dapple-grey stallion. The clouds never entirely left the bare hills in peace but today there were only a few that cast their spotty shadows as they continued north.

He adjusted his cap and satchel under the heat and was joined by Marina.

"Good morning, Bentley," she said cheerily.

"Is it 'good'?"

"Are you nervous?"

"Of course."

"I'm terrified."

"You'll be fine, you find study easy."

"I still have to study a lot to get the grades I do."

"I wasn't trying to say your effort was less than mine. I just find it hard to focus."

"Well, good luck anyway with the final results today. You'd have thought they could have sent them home and we find out with our parents rather than them being read out for everyone to hear."

"Yeah, and you'd also have thought they could have let our parents drop us off inside the school grounds."

"It's a summer tradition, making us walk the last few yards. Gets us out in the open air."

"You always see the positive side."

"Come on, the results will be posted up on the wall. Let's go in and get it over with. Are we going to Plymouth College next year or not?"

They walked down through the watchful granite gates and into the quad. Students were already coming out and punching the air, evidently pleased with their grades.

As Marina and Bentley approached, people glanced away. It was ominous. Jane Werrington glimpsed Marina and rushed up to her.

"Marina! Congrats—"

She cut off in mid-sentence the moment she saw Bentley next to her.

"Errm… the results are… well, you know where they are," and she walked off.

Inside, the hallway was a mass of students, swarming around the wooden notice board. As Marina and Bentley approached, the other students moved aside spontaneously to allow them to go to the front. They both noticed the odd behaviour. Marina found her name first and squealed at her straight 'A' grades. Then she turned her attention to Bentley.

"I can't seem to find my name," he said. "It should be here below Bentham, but there's nothing there."

Then someone pointed down at the bottom of the list to a separate area, cut off from the rest of the names by a red line.

"What's this?" said Marina.

"It's the list of those that failed," said Bentley.

"And how many are on that list?"

"Just me."

"Tough luck, Bentley," said one of the boys and patted him on the shoulder. One by one they gave him their condolences and left.

"Yeah, Bentley, hard luck," said the last student, walking away. Just Bentley and Marina were now left in the empty corridor.

"Come on, Bentley," said Marina, throwing her arm around him, "let's get outside and get some fresh air."

Bentley was visibly shaken.

"What happens now?" he asked.

Marina was stumped, she could never imagine such a scenario.

"I-I-I don't know what to say."

"It's all right," said Bentley calmly. "I know what will happen."

"You do?"

"It's as my mother always says, 'When one door closes another one opens.' I never really knew what it meant, but it makes sense now."

"Really?"

"Perhaps, it's destiny that I'm not meant to go to Plymouth College after all. The winds will carry me somewhere else, and it could even be better for me."

"Maybe," said Marina quietly.

"No one has died, I suppose," continued Bentley. "You've got to keep things in perspective and I still have my health. There's that to consider," and with that last line, he gathered his composure, straightened his tie and began to walk to class as if nothing had happened.

"It's true, no one has died," said Marina. "I'm impressed with your philosophical approach."

"What other approach is there to take? Tomorrow is another day. So long as my parents don't throw me out, I should be able to see myself through."

After lunch, they all congregated down in the playground by the rugby pitch. Bentley noticed that Britton was staring at him and he had the sense that his day of bad experiences wasn't entirely over.

Bentley and Marina went to a quiet corner under the cover of the chestnut trees, but they had sought peace and quiet in vain. Britton soon found them.

"So, it turns out you're the dumbest student in the school," taunted the bully.

"No, just the class," replied Bentley, not allowing Britton to gloat.

"He's brighter than you'll ever be," chipped in Marina, furious at the situation.

"I am not going to listen to you, Moses."

"What *is it* with your obsession about Marina being Jewish?" said Bentley.

"You can't ignore the facts," said Britton, looking more menacing than ever. "She's Jewish and there's nothing more to it.

"True, you can't ignore facts, no matter how uncomfortable," she replied, supremely calm and in control of the situation.

"What?" Britton tried to interrupt her.

"The truth of the matter is," Marina continued unhindered, "that I do *not* have Jewish ancestry."

Everyone drew closer, surprised by Marina's announcement.

"What? You? Not Jewish? Pull the other one," said Britton, waving a leg at her.

"No, I'm not Jewish, but as I've said before, I *do* have Jewish friends. Mrs Nathan, the caretaker at the synagogue lets me help her out there sometimes."

"Is that the lady who makes the challah bread?" asked Bentley.

"That's right," smiled Marina, "and apart from the bread she makes other amazing Jewish food, I love it as all Brits do!"

"I doubt that," huffed Britton.

"Fish and chips - brought here by the Jews," continued Marina, ignoring him. "Anyway, I have no Jewish blood. At least, not that I know of. What I *do know* is that I have Spanish ancestry. 'Hernan' is an anglicized version of 'Hernández'. *Capitán* Iago Hernández, in fact, of the Spanish Armada. He settled here after being imprisoned in Torquay."

"No way! You're lying!" said Britton.

"Am I? Are you sure you believe what you say? It's important to face the facts? Because one fact here that explains everything, Britton, is that *your* name comes from a persecuted minority, not mine."

Britton's face changed immediately. Bentley had never seen him look like that. Britton appeared lost, humiliated, as if a deep personal secret had just been revealed - and it had.

"What are you talking about?! There's no more British a name than *Britton*, or are you completely stupid?"

"Britton is from the name *Bretón*, in fact, 17th century French Huguenots—"

"Hugo what?" interrupted Bentley.

"Huguenots," answered Marina, "Protestants, persecuted in Catholic France. I looked it up, you obviously haven't. They came here in their tens of thousands, and 'Britton' is just one such Huguenot name. My mother knows the whole history, but you clearly don't. Nothing to be ashamed about though."

"So, he's a 'Hugo'?" said Bentley mockingly, holding back a laugh.

Britton clearly didn't like his new nickname.

Muffled giggles and gasps from the onlookers surrounded them while Britton came to terms with the fact he had been defeated at his own game. He was coming out in an involuntary sweat under the growing sense of disgrace.

Bentley drove home their advantage and chanted till his lungs burst, "Hugo, Hugo, Hugo"

Britton lifted his panic-stricken eyes and lunged at Marina, throwing her to the ground.

The act of violence enraged Bentley, who shoved Britton aside. As he helped Marina back to her feet, she shrieked. Britton charged at Bentley, screaming like an unleashed animal. He punched him hard on the right side of his face. Bentley collapsed on the ground, wounded. While he struggled to get his senses back, Britton heckled him as the other students closed in around them, chanting, "Fight! Fight! Fight!"

Britton turned round to calm their cheering. He was grinning from ear to ear. But that would be his downfall as in that pause Bentley sprang to his feet, putting all his energy into the end of his fist and connected it with Britton's chin. As the bully turned to confront his prey, he met the blow square on. He went flying backwards and crashed to the ground. His head landed with a thud against the large tree root. Britton was out cold. The cheering stopped at once.

"You've killed him!" cried one of them.

Bentley's molten-hot rage froze instantly. He had a sick feeling in the pit of his stomach, his head began to spin. He struggled to keep his balance. Marina took charge of the situation, "Call a teacher!"

The students backed off to let Britton get some air. The next thing they knew was that Britton was being lifted into the back of an ambulance, still unconscious. Bentley and Marina were summoned to the headmaster's office.

It was some time later that afternoon before the two of them re-emerged from Red House. Bentley's father was now with them. Marina was in tears and Bentley was on the verge.

"Expelled!" she managed to get the word out. "How could they expel you? Britton started it! And he hit you first! And then they expel you with just a few weeks left? What sense does it make?"

"Don't cry," said Bentley, but she couldn't help herself. "It's not your fault."

"Get your things, son. I'll wait for you in the car."

Bentley let go of Marina's hand, "I'll see you around."

He got into the passenger seat of the Jaguar XJS.

There was a brief silence. The car sat there. Bentley looked at his father, who was tapping the steering wheel pensively, staring straight ahead.

"Are you angry?" Bentley eventually plucked up the courage to ask him.

"Should I be? I suppose convention dictates I should. Well… I'm not. I know you were provoked, and you responded in self-defence. A bully played with fire and got burnt. It's unfortunate that it has come to this. He is still unconscious, but should recover later today, they say. But you mustn't let this expulsion consume you." He turned to look at his son, "do you hear me?"

"Yes, Father."

"One door closes and another one opens, as your mother is fond of saying. You'll see she's right. I know you to be a respectable, decent human being, and I am proud to call myself your father. The world is a better place with you in it, Chester, and no parent could ask for more."

The emotion welled up inside Bentley. He had never heard his father speak like that, but then he supposed that extreme circumstances called for extreme declarations.

His father eased the car into gear and the Jaguar pulled Bentley out of Forcastle College for the last time. He cast a glance over the yellow gorse and wild moor beyond and considered his uncertain future.

He passed his hand through his hair and his rebellious tuft folded down, and for once stayed there. Now it was only left to see which door his father had mentioned, would open for him. And as it turned out he would not have to wait long.

Bentley lay in his bed staring up at the ceiling, the full moon pouring in through his window. It was late and he had been there for hours his thoughts going round in circles and landing nowhere. His digital clock radio played music but the volume was almost imperceptible. He heard the song *Those were the days* and for a second recognised McCartney's voice from the Beatles but then paid it no more attention. He returned to thinking about nothing and everything, until finally his eyes closed and his body was able to relax.

When he opened his eyes he found himself in a dark place, the moonlight had gone. For some reason he felt strange as if things were not normal but he didn't know why. He was in a house but it wasn't his house. What was going on? Then he heard a dull sound. He walked down the dark narrow corridor feeling his way. A dim light beckoned him and the sound grew more distinct, it was McCartney's voice. Had the song brought him here? His legs began to drag. He wanted to enter the room but something was stopping him. The door began to close slowly. He pulled harder on his leaden legs bursting from the effort. He outstretched his hand in a desperate attempt to block the door, but it was no use. Before he was about to explode he woke up.

His chest was heaving, his pounding heart beating painfully against his ribs. He was covered in sweat. Then he gathered his thoughts and realised where he was. He relaxed and as his breath began to return to him, his tense body falling back into the mattress. "It was just a dream... just a dream," he whispered. For a belief moment he felt relieved that none of it had been real, but that didn't last long. It hadn't been anything like he had experienced before. Had it just been a dream? Was it just because of what had happened with Britton? Bentley felt even more unsettled than before he had fallen asleep. What was happening to him?

"GOD BLEW AND THEY SCATTERED" 1588

Just as the Spanish thought the darkness had become a calm, safe place, Lord Howard gave the signal and the ghost ships, under the guidance of Young, Prowse and their skeleton crews were sent down the wind and into the dead of the night.

Below decks Moses rested in his bunk, unaware that Mendez was approaching silently. The other sailors were above, straining their eyes in the blind darkness that stared back at them, waiting for the midnight attack to commence.

Mendez reached his hand up over Moses' chest toward his tunic in an attempt to steal the object which he guarded for Drake, but the helmsman was not asleep.

Moses took hold of the thief's hand and flipped out of the bunk. He twisted Mendez's arm round and forced it up against his back. Mendez felt as if his arm was about to snap. He was trapped. Moses yelled up for assistance when a flash of flames lit up the night sky as shouting broke the night silence.

Sparks grew into a warm glow, as flames jumped up the ropes in fits and starts.

Mendez took advantage of the brief distraction and threw himself backwards, smashing Moses against a wooden beam and knocking him to the ground. Now free from Moses' grip he turned for his sword.

"Stand where you are!" shouted Moses, his sword already drawn, "if ya do not want cold steel in your limbs." Mendez froze just a few steps from his sword. He weighed his options.

Within moments a strong fire had built and then burst into a lurid inferno, blazing into the black sky. The Spanish were not easy prey though and had put up a defensive line of picquet vessels to draw the fireships off from their vulnerable fleet.

"They are pulling the fireships away, my Lord!" said one of the sailors to his Admiral. They could hear the Spanish sailors cheering now.

Lord Howard turned to hide his anger and sharp disappointment, "It has come to naught!" he hissed to himself. But then an explosion ripped through the night. Lord Howard turned round in desperate hope and there followed another and then another fitful release of energy, metal and flames that erupted in all directions. The towing vessels lost control of their burning cargo as the guns inside the hellburners began blowing apart.

Mendez lunged forward for his sword. Moses was quick to react and caught him before he could remove his sword from its scabbard. He pushed him into the hull, gashing his head against the timber. Mendez fell in a crumpled heap.

Moses waited to see if he would rise to his feet, but Mendez was unconscious. Moses smiled to himself, almost having enjoyed the cat and mouse game with the Portuguese sailor and then rejoined the men above deck.

Then it happened - panic set in, and the order was given for the Spanish fleet to weigh anchor, cut cables and put to sea. As the great galleons and their lesser consorts began to lurch and move away, the cheering now began on the English ships. One Spanish vessel banked on the shore and two caught fire while the rest made away.

Lord Howard looked at a sailor beside him, "Tomorrow we end this enterprise!"

Day broke and Lord Howard found the Spanish widely dispersed.

Mendez appeared late that morning above deck, his head bandaged and pride damaged. He kept a safe distance from Moses; the helmsman knew his intentions and Mendez knew there would be repercussions once the Spanish had been seen off. He would have to be wary. He had failed aboard ship and would have to make his move as soon as they were on dry land.

"What happened to his head?" Drake asked Moses.

"Must have fallen out of his bunk with all the excitement last night," grinned Moses.

Before Drake could comment, Lord Howard gave the order to attack. With the *Ark Royal* at the head of the fleet, the English engaged in a full assault against an Armada in disarray.

The English cannons fired constant volleys, as the Spanish ships beat back to assist the Duke's ship *San Martín*, which received some two hundred impacts, before five brave galleons confronted the entire English fleet, as they awaited reinforcements to slowly arrive.

"The time is now, if we wish to stop the Dukes of Sidonia and Parma shaking hands," said Drake through gritted teeth. His gun crews below deck fired without intermission, "I know this feeling, Moses. Close quarters with them. Senhor Mendez! Keep them cannon spewin' fire!"

Mendez nodded and relayed the order below. He then took up his position again behind Moses. Moses stared at the Portuguese man and as he turned to look him in the eye, he saw him staring not at him but at Drake, who was in front of the helm. Mendez looked hypnotized, then he realised Moses was looking at him and woke from his daze. Unable to deflect Moses' attention, he went below decks to avoid any interrogation. He was convinced his cover was blown and Moses fully suspected him for what he was. His life was now in grave danger. He would have to follow through with his mission whether the English were successful or not.

Drake looked across to the Spanish target as the cannon shot smashed through the hull and water gushed in through its path of destruction. A fierce fight now ensued as English cannons engaged in a continuous rain of shot, driving home their advantage with emboldened tactics amid the Spanish disorder.

The Spanish vessels received a merciless punishment. The shot pierced their hulls, leaving gaping wounds that would slowly pull many of them to the bottom of the sea in the days that would follow. Smaller Spanish craft were forced to round up the larger ones and bring them to the front. Out to sea, away from the coast, English ships preyed upon their solitary Spanish counterparts by encircling them and firing upon the defenceless vessels that had clearly finished their ordinance.

"The evening has come, and night will soon fall," said Howard, "the Armada is being pressed leeward onto the Zeeland sandbars. Our work is done here. There can be no better end for us."

"But my Lord," said the helmsman, "the wind is changing!"

"No! This cannot be! They will escape at the very last!"

The disaster that was about to befall the Armada was averted by the unseasonable weather and contrary winds that had been Catholic Spain's antagonist until that very moment of unexpected deliverance.

"We have done all we can today," stated Howard, hiding his discontent. "Tomorrow we must ensure they do not return. If we do this small duty, then England is preserved... this time."

"Mendez?" called Drake, take your spyglass and tell me what you see.

Mendez picked up the long spyglass and looked out to the Spanish fleet. A jury seemed to be assembled and a group were being tried. Treason? thought Mendez. Then one man was singled out. He seemed to remonstrate his innocence but was strung up and then his body placed down in a small craft that was towed by the Duke's, a warning to the others.

"Don Cristóbal de Ávila," whispered Mendez.

"Ya knew him?" said Moses.

"Heard of him," corrected Mendez.

"Well, ya won't be hearin' anymore of him now."

"What is their game, Drake?" asked Lord Howard.

"It seems they are trimming their sails. They want us to engage."

"It is their only hope for returning to the Channel and back to either Parma's army or home. Send up the order to trim our sails. We go no further."

"Trim the sails!" went up the call, and all hands tied the canvas up, slowing the ships to a standstill.

The Armada waited in the distance, the wind pushing them ever northwards. The two fleets waited idly as the day wore on until the decision was finally taken by the Duke of Medina de Sidonia.

"What's that falling into the water?" Moses asked his captain.

"Horses and mules. He's throwing those beasts overboard to save on supplies and weight no doubt. They're going to sail the north route."

"They'll be beaten to the coast," said Moses.

"The tempests will take the hindmost, they will," forebode Drake.

Then the Spanish sails came down one last time from their beams and the fleet began to turn.

"We shall follow them leeward until their trajectory is a sure thing," commanded Howard.

And so, the English fleet carried up the east coast until they reached Scotland, where Lord Howard finally gave the order to desist in the chase.

The Queen's ships shot off a great volume of ordinance for joy - the men would see home again.

"So, we've carried the day!" said Lord Howard's helmsman. "They're going North About."

"The westerly winds have seen to it. God blew and they scattered," said Lord Howard. "The North Sea hath shortened our labour."

On the *Revenge*, Drake and Moses shook hands, "*Venit, Vidit, Fugit,*" said Drake, "They came, they saw, they fled."

"They are prisoners to the coast now," said Moses.

"There will be no noble family in Spain that does not lose a man on the return voyage," said Drake.

Providence would prove him right.

- XXIX -

COMING ASHORE
1588

"I will admit to you, Moses," said Drake as he stepped ashore and made his way through the cheering crowds at Plymouth's Sutton harbour, "it was the greatest conflict that never was. And if God is not a Protestant then he was at least not willing to stop the will of men defeating his representatives on Earth, namely King Felipe and the Pope. Their prayers were not answered and ours were."

"Perhaps God does not listen to prayers then, if that is the case," added Moses.

"As I always say: God only helps those who help themselves."

Moses did not reply, only contemplated his captain's words from a distance as he swung his master's bag over one shoulder and stuffed a few small belongings inside his tunic.

"Let us be gone from these crowds," continued Drake, "and back to the Minerva Inn. Sleep is not far away, and I require some ale to settle me head." He slapped his faithful helmsman on the back.

"You captained well, Sir Francis," said Mendez, who carried along the cobble streets two steps behind them. Moses turned and scowled at the man bringing up the rear. They had unfinished business, but that would be attended to do at a later moment.

"There are those that made it a more difficult task than it should have been," answered Drake, looking across

167

knowingly at Moses. Mendez knew Drake was referring to him but took no notice.

They turned a corner and walked up the small incline, the street lined by grubby white-washed cottages. Halfway up was a warm light filtering onto the street, from wherein the carousing was louder than usual. Mendez saw Moses reach inside his tunic for something. He suddenly pushed past Moses. He had a mission to fulfill and this was his moment. He had never trusted Moses. "Sir Francis!" he called out.

The robust man turned slowly, his painful gait evident, but it was time enough for Moses. As Drake faced Mendez, the Portuguese soldier hastily thrust a case-knife into him. But as Mendez looked up expecting to see the dying eyes of the bearded Drake, he instead gazed into the crazed eyes of Moses, who had come between them. Mendez tried to retract the blade but it was stuck inside Moses.

The next thing he felt was a burning pain of sharp steel piercing his rib cage, leaving him incapable of drawing breath. Moses released the grip on his knife as Mendez crumpled to the ground, taking Moses' blade with him. Drake turned his helmsman to one side to inspect him and saw Mendez's large blade still hanging from his tunic, but Moses was still standing straight. There weren't even signs of blood.

"What in the name of—" exclaimed Drake.

Moses saw the dying Mendez hold up a hand for support, his eyes now knowing his last seconds were upon him. Moses bent down to hear what he had to say. But Mendez said nothing, instead he groped desperately inside Moses' tunic to see the object he had tried in vain to take aboard ship. He had to see Drake's talisman, the treasure that Moses had guarded so dearly; had it been worth his sacrifice to try and take it from him? Finally, he clasped his hand on the object and pulled it.

When his eyes fell upon the mysterious object his face frowned and broke into a pathetic whimper, "Noooo!" he cried.

"Me Lord!" gasped Drake. "Of all the things on God's Earth! I had forgotten I had entrusted that to your keeping."

Moses handed the object back to Drake.

"No," said the great man. "It's yours. I doubt it'll ever be useful to you in the future, but it saved your life, ensured our victory and that is worth something. Keep it man."

"It's a handsome prize, me Lord," said Moses. And they both grinned. Then they looked back down at Mendez.

"Spies? You said," Drake hissed, as the Portuguese man struggled with the last few short breaths left inside him.

"It's *Señor* Mendez, isn't it? Not *Senhor* with an 'h'," said Moses, seeing the situation clearly now. "You're Spanish, not Portuguese."

Mendez gave a slight smile of recognition and then his face was seized by agonising pain. He went rigid and then his body relaxed completely, and he was gone.

"I never liked him," said Moses.

"And I never trusted him. You should always trust your instincts. I'll get the landlord to clear this away. Let's go inside and drink to our victory."

They pushed their way inside to be received by wild ovations. Laurels were placed on their heads as Drake was invited to write his name and the date up on the inn wall. The applause calmed briefly, and Drake addressed them,

"You all know the news, so all we need to know now is, where were we before I left?" The revellers burst out laughing and cheering.

The landlord stepped forward as silence descended in the claustrophobic bar, and he slapped a tankard of ale into Drake's hand.

"Exactly! Me hearties!" declared Drake, and then the drinking started up again.

169

"Come on, Moses!" They turned to the back of the bar. The wall of people standing there moved aside, revealing a bowling alley. "As I was saying, Moses - plenty of time to thrash the Spaniards!" He took a swig on his ale and cast a wooden ball down the narrow lane, scattering the skittles in all directions.

PART THREE
- MURDER -

XXX

THE CASE OF ASHER WORTH,
Plymouth - 1939

Account by Chief Constable Chapman

First Entry

As I approach the day of my retirement from the Plymouth Borough Police Force, I have found that I have been reminiscing, looking back at the cases that I have worked on, some solved, some unsolved, some long forgotten, now just meaningless names and scribbles languishing in yellowing files at the back of my office.

I have lived through the Great War and been moved by the loss of many of my colleagues who fought in it. I have witnessed the results of horrific crimes. But no matter how many cases I have worked on, or how many years I have left to live, I shall never forget the details of one case, which haunts me to this very day and sends a shiver snaking down my spine, and that is the case of Asher Worth. It was one of my first cases as Chief Constable which makes it particularly memorable.

Asher Worth was a fine gentleman, or at least he appeared to be. He lived in one of the rather grand residences in Plymouth. I saw him once, emerging from behind the wrought iron gates which protected the street's residents from unsavoury characters. Sometimes I would pass him as I made my way to the police station. He cut a fine figure in his morning suit with its smart waistcoat and pocket watch, and his high collar was always immaculately starched and pressed. It matched his prematurely white hair and beard.

On Sundays, he was usually accompanied by his stunning younger wife and a child whose bonnet and smock were equally as dazzling as her father's collar. When she toddled beside her mother, she appeared for all the world like a little angel and bore no resemblance to my own two ruffians who could dirty their clothes just by looking at them.

Mr Worth worked at the Plymouth bank, a fact which gave him immediate prestige. He was one of the many white-haired gentlemen that moved with an air of secrecy behind its walls. But whatever they did, they did it well and the bank had a good reputation with a rapidly growing clientele. Until the 'incident' as I shall refer to it for now.

I had just got used to my new role as Chief Constable when I received a visit from the bank manager, Mr Ball. He was aptly named, as his coat seemed to stretch over his round stomach, creating a tent-like space where a small child could easily hide. He approached my desk nervously, removed his hat and said that he wished to report a missing person.

"A missing person?" I echoed, reaching for my notebook and pencil. "And who might that be?"

He ran one hand across his balding head and twisted his gloves as he glanced around.

"Well, it's rather a delicate matter, sir. One of my employees, a Mr Smith, has failed to report for work since last week."

"Is there any chance that he could be ill? I hear that there's a nasty bout of influenza here in Plymouth"

He cleared his throat. "No chance at all. I went to visit his wife and she assured me that she hasn't seen him either."

"A marital dispute, perhaps?"

Mr Ball took a step closer to the desk and leaned over until his face was uncomfortably close to mine. "I don't believe it was a marital dispute, sir," he whispered, "you see, he has gone missing with a substantial sum of money which was owed to the bank." There was perspiration on Mr Ball's brow, he drew a silk handkerchief from his pocket and mopped it, still glancing furtively around the office.

"Come with me, Mr Ball. I believe we may need to talk somewhere a little more private." I led him into the interview room which always seemed to have a faint whiff of desperation about it with its scuffed walls and chipped table. But Mr Ball immediately looked more at ease and took a seat without invitation. I sat opposite.

"I'd like you to tell me exactly when you last saw Mr Smith and the details of the missing money."

Mr Ball hesitated and began…

"I saw Mr Smith last Monday. He came into the bank as usual and dealt with a few clients. I remember that because as I passed by his room, he was talking to Mrs Reeves and as you are aware, sir, she does tend to shout. It's impossible not to hear all her business."

"And then?"

"I didn't see him again. I wasn't concerned at first, believing him to be ill but when he still hadn't returned by Friday, I set about finding out why. That's when I discovered from my employees that he had recently received an order to collect a substantial sum of money from one of our debtors in Cornwall."

"And who issued this order?"

"Mr Asher Worth."

I scribbled down Mr Worth's name and underlined it.

"Naturally, I became worried and immediately went to Mr Smith's home to see if he was there. That's when his wife informed me that she hadn't set eyes on him since he had left for Cornwall. She thought he was still on business and wasn't overly concerned. So, I telephoned the office where the transaction was meant to have taken place and the solicitor there confirmed that the money had been handed over to Mr Smith, as planned."

"So, he's been missing for a week?"

Mr Ball nodded.

"May I ask why it has taken you so long to report this incident, Mr Ball?"

Mr Ball looked sheepish, "I was hoping that he would appear with the money, sir. I have no wish to create a false alarm, a scandal. Whatever will the people of the town think, if I tell them that we have failed to protect their money?" He mopped his brow again. "We'll lose customers!"

I sighed, empathising with his situation and immediately thinking of my own paltry savings which were also housed with his institution. However, I couldn't complain, as I now received a Chief Constable's wage and no longer had to struggle quite as much.

"Am I right in thinking that Mr Smith travelled to Cornwall, unaccompanied, to collect this debt?"

"Yes, sir."

"A dangerous job for any man, wouldn't you say?"

Mr Ball didn't reply.

"I will have to make some enquiries with our colleagues in Cornwall. But I'll need a full description of Mr Smith. And details of the debtor and of the solicitor."

"Of course."

I recorded the details and stood up ready to escort Mr Ball from the room, but he didn't join me. I noticed that he was perspiring again.

"Was there something else, Mr Ball?"

He hesitated before he answered, "No, nothing important, sir." His mumbling manner bothered me, but I let it go at the time.

I bid him farewell, reassuring him that the matter would be dealt with discreetly. Then I telephoned my colleagues in Cornwall to see what they knew. A man with money would soon be spotted there.

XXXI

THE CASE OF ASHER WORTH

Second Entry, 1939

I remember that some particularly unseasonal weather seemed to be affecting the telephone lines that day. There was more crackling on the line than on a raging fire, but I managed to convey the urgency of the situation to Cornwall. I also questioned the solicitor, Mr Englebright, who confirmed that the debtor had handed over the money to Mr Smith in a patterned carpet bag in his offices.

A day later I received a return call. A man's body had been found dumped in an abandoned house located not far from the solicitor's office. There was no trace of the money. There was a request for the body to be formally identified and I remember thinking that after such a long time it would be wise for someone other than Mrs Smith to do the honours.

When I informed Mr Ball of his employee's demise and the money's disappearance, he blanched and began to shake. I thought that he was about to cry until his eyes grew dark and his mouth set in a grim line. He banged his fist on his desk making a pile of papers topple and then swept them aside where they drifted slowly to the floor like snowflakes. Then he stood up and pointed at me.

"It is your duty, Chief Constable to ensure that whoever committed this murder and theft is found and receives the harshest punishment possible. The money must be returned.

The good name of the bank is at stake! We cannot have our customers transferring their money to Bristol, it will be our ruin. I need this to be solved as quickly and as discreetly as possible and I think you should start by questioning Mr Asher Worth."

There was a strange expression on Mr Ball's face which reminded me of his manner at the station when he had seemed reluctant to leave. Something was clearly playing on his mind.

"Mr Worth *was* the person who gave the orders to Mr Smith to collect the money from Cornwall…" said Mr Ball.

"Are you implying that Mr Worth was somehow involved in the theft and murder?"

"I am, officer, because not three months ago, Mr Worth came to me in a desperate state and asked me for a substantial loan." Mr Ball looked triumphant.

"May I ask the nature of the loan?"

"He said it was for life-saving medical treatment for his daughter. But I didn't believe him."

"So, you refused?"

"Yes."

"What led you to believe he was lying?"

Mr Ball went red, "Just instinct. I believe he is living beyond his means, with that fancy house and his pocket watch. He seems to be spending more money than he earns. I thought that perhaps he was in debt to some money lenders, not the bank of course."

"And you didn't check with his wife, or friends to verify the story of his daughter?"

He shook his head, his chin wobbling slightly.

I felt my eyebrows rise involuntarily. Mr Ball noticed and cleared his throat. "Anyway, he hasn't mentioned it since and I thought no more of it, until the other day, when I learned that the money was missing and that he had given the order for its collection. He's the only person who knew where that money would be and at what time, and the only person I can think of who has a motive. He could easily have arranged to have the money intercepted. I wouldn't be surprised to learn that he's in cahoots with a gang in Cornwall."

I thought of Asher Worth and failed to see the same man that Mr Ball was describing. But if the police force has taught me one thing, it is that criminals can come in the most ingenious of disguises.

"You didn't raise these suspicions when you first reported the theft," I said, observing him closely. "Why not?"

"I didn't wish to seem as if I was singling him out, what with him being Jewish and everything. Their community is small but influential, and I do not wish to appear to be discriminating, because I assure you that I am not. But I have to say what I have to say. Justice must be done."

"I understand your concerns, Mr Ball. Naturally, it makes sense to begin my enquiries with Asher Worth, seeing as he gave Mr Smith the orders, although you must understand that I need to speak to all your employees, not just him. And if Mr Worth is guilty of this crime then never doubt that we will make him pay." Looking back now, those are words that I wish I had never said.

- XXXII -

THE CASE OF ASHER WORTH

Third Entry, 1939

Eager to avoid any speculation and gossip, I arranged for a colleague and myself to conduct the employee interviews at the bank. I chose Jarvis, a rather young constable who I had taken under my wing. He had an incredible eye for detail, but his lack of confidence meant that he often held back his observations. I decided that this case would be perfect as I needed someone like him, and it would boost his self-assurance. I also believed that he would keep the finer details of the case to himself, as I trusted his discretion.

Jarvis had the use of the room next to Mr Ball's, which I had requisitioned for our interviews. The plan was for Mr Ball to fetch the employees, one by one, and bring them for questioning. Jarvis began with one of the clerks and I began with Mr Asher Worth.

As Asher Worth entered the office, I observed him closely. I must admit that he looked more tired than usual, the dark shadows beneath his eyes perhaps indicating a lack of sleep, but other than that he appeared to be in fine form. He sat with his back straight and his hands calmly placed in his lap.

"Mr Worth," I began, "you're aware that one of your colleagues, Mr William Smith, has failed to appear for work since last week."

"Yes, sir, I am."

"I'd like you to tell me exactly what happened and what discussions took place between you on the last day that you saw him."

Mr Worth didn't appear unnerved by this request. He stroked his beard for a moment as if in contemplation before he answered."

"Well, Mr Smith came into work as usual, last Monday. I remember him commenting on the cloudy morning and then I didn't see him again until I asked him to see me."

"For what purpose?"

"I needed him to go to Cornwall, to recover a sum of money from one of our debtors. It was all arranged; he was to go to the offices of Mr Englebright, the solicitor, on the following morning at 9 a.m. and meet Mr Danby, who would hand over what was owed. Mr Englebright would then witness that transaction and he would return immediately to Plymouth."

"But neither he nor the money appeared?"

"No."

"And have you seen him since?"

"No, sir."

"Do you have any idea where he or the money might be?"

"No, sir."

"Mr Worth, I have to ask you a delicate question now. Did you recently ask Mr Ball for a loan?"

"I did."

"For what purpose?"

Mr Worth looked distressed for a moment, then composed himself with a deep breath. "For my daughter's medical treatment."

The sum mentioned was vast. "May I ask what treatment would cost so much?"

"My daughter has an unknown illness, which is sapping her strength with merciless haste. The only possible chance of a cure lies in London. I need money for my wife to take her, for accommodation and the treatment."

"I see, and your doctor is?"

"Doctor Garth."

I made a note of his name.

"And now that this loan has been refused…"

Mr Worth raised his chin slightly, "My daughter will die!"

I tried to detect any sense of sorrow in his words but could find none. I was surprised by his stoicism. It was time to truly test his reaction.

"And do you not have any funds? If you don't mind my saying you do live in a rather grand house…"

"I received an inheritance," he interrupted. "Money, and a few heirlooms. My house is also up for sale in the hope a buyer will come forward, however, the market has grown stagnant of late, but I had to explore every avenue open to me."

"I see," I scribbled down this additional information.

"Mr Worth, I need to inform you that your colleague, Mr Smith, was found dead just yards from the office where he received the money!"

Asher Worth's eyes widened in apparent shock. I noticed that he gripped his fist slightly.

"And there was no trace of the money," I continued, "which leads us to the obvious conclusion that he was robbed and murdered, or should I say murdered and then robbed."

Mr Worth sat in silence.

"I'm going to ask you a question, Mr Worth, one that we will be asking everyone in the employ of this bank. And, I'd like you to think very carefully before you give me an answer. Did you have anything to do with this incident?"

"No, sir, I did not." He looked straight into my eyes as he spoke.

"Do you know who did?"

"I do not."

"Can you think of anyone with a motive?"

"No, sir. Mr Smith was well liked."

"Thank you, Mr Worth. You may go, for now. We may need to speak to you again soon."

He rose almost regally, but when he reached the door, he turned to look at me with an expression in his eyes, which I could not fathom but will never forget.

It was a tiring day which was not helped by Mr Ball loitering in the corridor between interviews. I could see his agitated shadow passing backwards and forwards through the frosted glass pane. Whenever anyone came out, he would poke his head through the door and ask me how things were going, even though I told him each time that I could not divulge any information.

By the end of the day, Jarvis and I had spoken to everyone. When we reached the station, we shut ourselves away in the interview room with a cup of tea and a slice of Jarvis' mother's fruit cake, to compare notes.

"I haven't come up with anything, sir," he said, clearly disappointed. "Most of these employees are the same; they're just family men, busy making a living and going home to their wives and children at the end of the day. Keeping their heads above water. But there is something that bothers me…"

"What's that?" I noticed that Jarvis was becoming hesitant again, "Really, Jarvis, if there's anything that you would like to share, even if it's just a hunch, then spit it out - preferably without any crumbs!"

"Well, sir, there is a general sense of unease surrounding Asher Worth. People don't trust him. People don't really like him."

Jarvis had interviewed many of the clerks who had worked with Asher Worth before his promotion.

"Any comments in particular?"

"Yes, he doesn't fit in. He works after hours. He has risen surprisingly quickly to a position that would normally take years to attain. And everyone commented on his house. Do you think it's jealousy, sir?"

"One thing I have come to understand about us English, young Jarvis, is that we despise success and will put it down to any number of heinous injustices, apart from the obvious explanation - plain hard work. In the case of Asher Worth, the simple justification could well be the fact that he's Jewish. What I am certainly convinced of though, is I have to pay a visit to the doctor."

"Feeling unwell, sir?"

"Fit as a fiddle, Jarvis - not my doctor - Asher Worth's, or rather his daughter's doctor."

"You've lost me now, sir," he frowned.

"First thing tomorrow come with me and I'll explain on the way."

Dr Garth was a tiny man with a slightly stooped posture and hooded eyes. This gave him the appearance of a small bird of prey. He wore a long white coat which swamped his tiny frame. Jarvis and I towered above him, but he seemed unnerved by our presence and motioned for us to sit down in two worn leather chairs, the kind with studs along the edges and high backs, which could have belonged in a medieval court.

"How can I be of help?"

"We'd like to ask you about a patient of yours - the daughter of Mr Asher Worth.

"Annie Worth? Of course, what would you like to know?"

"The state of her health."

"Not good, not good, poor child!" Dr Garth shuffled to a tall wooden cabinet which was crammed with files, haphazardly stacked. Miraculously, he seemed to locate the child's file within seconds and pulled it out from its place without disturbing the others. When he returned to his desk, he opened the file and consulted it briefly before looking up. "She last visited me three weeks ago."

"And, how was she?"

"She had a slight cough, some wheezing…"

"Related to her illness?"

"Yes, yes, indeed. There is really very little to be done for the poor child, although if the parents were able to find the money, they would at least have a glimmer of a chance in London."

"And that treatment is not available here, in Plymouth?"

"No. A colleague of mine moved to London two years ago. He's working on a new treatment. It's had a good success rate, I believe, but unfortunately, Annie Worth will not be among those children cured."

Jarvis looked moved and I felt the same, but I reminded myself that we were here to confirm Annie Worth's illness and in doing so prove Asher Worth's motive for the murder of Samuel Smith.

"Doctor, can I ask *when* Annie was first diagnosed with this illness and *when* you told the family of the treatment?"

The doctor nodded and consulted his file again, flicking back through the pages with his long fingers. "Three months ago," he announced. "I must admit, I was very surprised that Mr Worth hasn't managed to raise the funds."

"How so?" I asked.

"Well, I always believed he was a gentleman of money. His family was wealthy, although there is some speculation about where they got their money from. But one day, Mrs Worth came to see me with Annie. And when I asked if they had managed to raise the funds, she told me that her husband had asked for a loan from the bank, which had been refused, but she knew that there was a way he could raise the money, she just had to convince him to do it."

"Have you any idea what she was referring to?"

"No, I was very puzzled. Still am to tell you the truth." He shook his head sadly and closed Annie's file. "Is there anything else I can help you with, gentlemen?"

"No, thank you, you've been very helpful."

He accompanied us to the door and then closed it behind us. We hurried down the narrow corridor to the main entrance where the receptionist sat behind a ridiculously large desk. She smiled as we approached, and Jarvis stopped suddenly. "You go ahead, sir, I need to make an appointment. I think I might be coming down with that lurgy that's going around."

I left him to it and stood outside in the fresh air. It was beginning to rain, a fine drizzle which coated my uniform in tiny drops. I stayed where I was, not caring as only one thing occupied my mind - that Asher Worth *did* have a motive for the murder of Samuel Smith.

- XXXIII -

THE CASE OF ASHER WORTH

Fourth Entry, 1939

Jarvis was indeed ill the following day and sent word that he would be staying at home. This was most inconvenient as I was hoping to take him along to question Asher Worth again. I was just about to leave, alone, when we received news that a man was being held for questioning in London in connection with the murder of Samuel Smith. No more details were given, only that the officers concerned had requested my presence. I had little desire to travel to London, wishing to stay close to Asher Worth, but packed a small bag and set off to begin the tedious train journey. I was eager to hear what the man had to say.

It was late when I arrived in London. I went directly to the address I had been given for my lodgings and after unpacking and eating a hearty casserole, I headed to the police station, keen to meet and question the man. I was met by the Chief Constable in charge of the case, who, although surprised by my late appearance, was keen to share his knowledge so far.

The man who had been detained had been aboard the Plymouth to London train and was rather the worse for wear with drink. He was sitting beside a fearless elderly lady who was travelling to London to visit her daughter. She happened to comment on the fine, unusual carpet bag which he carried with him. The man had then foolishly told her that he had just received an easy windfall, a quick job for a large reward which would see him out of poverty for the rest of his life. He was about to show her the contents, but then slowly leaned back in his seat and fell silent, one leg firmly anchoring the bag to the train floor. The lady, noticing that he had blood on his clothes and taking advantage of his slumber, boldly opened the bag and saw a rather large sum of money, neatly bundled into tight rolls. She then quickly alerted the guard. So, when the man awoke at the next stop and got off, the guard followed, informed the police and the man was pursued and arrested

"And how do you know that this carpet bag is the very same, which was stolen from Samuel Smith?" I asked.

"We discovered a ring with Mr Smith's initials inside," smiled the officer. "It seems that the thief was keen to rob the dead in more ways than one.

I asked if I could question the man and was led to a rather squalid cell. It was a Victorian building and the walls were so thick that I doubted any prisoner could ever have escaped, even if they had scraped away for a lifetime. The corridor felt damp and a sour stench hung in the air. Sensing my distaste, the Chief Constable opened the cell, cuffed the prisoner and led us back out into a small room where at least I could breathe without choking.

The man had clearly slept off his alcohol and was wide awake, his dark eyes darted from side to side and he sniffed loudly.

"I don't know what I'm here for!" he said.

"I've read you your rights, Mr Rook, so don't play the innocent with me," said Chief Constable Davies, pushing the man down onto one of the three chairs round the table. "You've been charged with the murder of Mr Samuel Smith and the theft of a carpet bag full of money! This wouldn't be your first theft, would it? And I do believe they call you *The*

Magpie - a great play on your name but also apt for your love of shiny things!"

The Magpie shuffled in his seat and looked away. "I ain't done nuffin!" he mumbled.

"I'd be careful with those double negatives if I were you," said Davies. The Magpie looked confused.

"Oh, never mind," said Davies. "Chief Constable Chapman, would you like to do the honours?"

I took a seat opposite The Magpie and looked at him sternly. "Do you understand what you've been charged with, Mr Rook?"

"Yeah, yeah, the murder of some old geezer and nicking his bag full of money." The Magpie sat back in his chair and looked at me challengingly. "You can't prove nuffin!"

"I'm afraid we can. You had the man's bag in your possession, and it contained the exact amount of money stolen. There is blood on your clothes. You even bragged to a fellow passenger. What were your words exactly? 'It was a quick and easy job'."

The Magpie licked his lips and frowned.

"Who told you that Mr Smith would be carrying so much money?" asked Davies.

I noticed that The Magpie looked thoughtful for a while and then he smiled suddenly.

"Were you working alone?" prodded Chief Constable Davies.

The Magpie looked down at his handcuffs and then up at Davies. "Maybe I was, maybe I wasn't, but what good will it do me if I snitch?"

"You're going to be locked up for this for a very long time, whether or not you confess!" Davies told him. We have a witness that saw you in that very street at that very time."

I looked up sharply - Davies hadn't mentioned this to me, he was bluffing.

The Magpie looked worried. He began to jiggle his leg up and down. "Look, I only meant to cut him up a bit and take the money. I was told to do what needed to be done!"

"Told by who?"

Again, The Magpie glanced to one side, buying time.

"What's in it for me if I tell?"

"Mr Rook," said Davies before I could stop him, "if you were working with someone, we'd like to know. We could reduce your sentence. After all, why should you be the only one to pay for the crime if there were more of you involved?"

"We…" Davies was about to speak again, but I raised a hand to silence him.

"Mr Rook," I took over. "Were you working with someone else?"

He hesitated, looked down once again at his handcuffs and then raised his eyes to mine, "Yes, I was!" he said firmly.

It was a long night. The Magpie's answers were evasive and convoluted. He seemed to enjoy toying with us. I felt ready to snap yet knew that if I showed any signs of weakness, he would take advantage of it. He played for time; he asked for water saying he was parched, then he needed a lengthy toilet break. Eventually, however, we managed to obtain a confession, as our depriving him of sleep weakened him of his resolve to resist.

He claimed to have been approached by a friend who knew someone in need of his services. This person did not wish to be named but would meet in person at the King's Arms to give him the details. He met the man who he had never seen before and was told that someone would be coming out of the solicitor's office with a large sum of money. That man was to be stopped and robbed and the bag taken directly to an address in London where the stranger would meet him.

"What did he look like? This man?"

"I don't know really. It was quite dark so I couldn't see too clearly. He seemed well-to-do; wore a fancy hooded coat. Tall, dark-haired with a beard and a nice pocket watch too, I saw it when he checked the time as I approached."

"A pocket-watch, you say? Would you be able to identify this man?"

"Oh yes," he said. "Definitely."

"Then tomorrow you'll accompany Chief Constable Davies and myself to Plymouth to identify him."

"Any chance I can get some kip now?" asked The Magpie, "all this questioning takes it out of a man."

"I'll take you back to your cell now," agreed Davies, "Then, in the morning we'll go over your statement one last time before heading to Plymouth."

Davies and I sat drinking a cup of tea. I felt exhausted, not only from the journey but from the questioning and the knowledge that when I returned, I would have to arrest Asher Worth and place him in an identity parade. Everything pointed to his involvement with the murder - his request for money for his daughter's treatment, his wife's comment that she knew there was 'a way', and The Magpie's description of the man he had met. All that was left was his formal identification. My heart sank.

"You've got a suspect then, for this collaborator?" said Davies.

I nodded. "I have. He works for the bank. He recently asked his manager for a loan, for his sick child. He was desperate for the money."

"Desperate enough to arrange a murder, it seems," yawned Davies. He drained the dregs of his tea. "Right then, I'm calling it a night. The missus will lock the front door if I'm much later." He laughed.

I made my way back to my lodgings, only to find that the bed was as lumpy as my grandmother's custard, God bless her. I slept regardless.

- XXXIV -

THE CASE OF ASHER WORTH

Fifth Entry, 1939

I returned to Plymouth the following day accompanied by
Chief Constable Davies and with The Magpie handcuffed to
me. This was most unpleasant as every jolt of the train
carriage threw me against him. I hoped that he wouldn't dirty
my frockcoat. He was placed in a cell at the police station.
Jarvis was nowhere to be seen but had reported for duty and
then gone on police business - where to, nobody knew. A
group of us headed for the Worth residence without him.

When we arrived, we were unable to make the approach
that we would have wanted. Instead, we had to stand
impotently at the gates until a kind neighbour unlocked them
for us with trembling hands. She directed us to Asher
Worth's house then retreated to the safety of her front porch.

I rang the doorbell and waited. There was no reply. I
banged on the door loudly enough to wake the dead. Then, I
bent down and pushed the shiny brass letter box open until I
could see into the hallway. There was a suitcase on the
bottom stair. "Mr Worth, open the door please!" Nothing
stirred, although I was sure that he must be in there. "Mr
Worth," I repeated, "open the door! Please. Otherwise, we
shall be forced to break it down."

"Right - in we go!" I stood back as two of my constables
broke down the door, which was no mean feat given the

strength and quality of its construction. There was no sign of him downstairs, so we ran up the stairs and onto the first landing where we paused. Instinct told me to continue up onto the second floor.

The doors were all shut, I stood at the top of the stairs and indicated for my men to check the bedrooms. "Mr Worth?" I called. There was no reply and the bedrooms were empty which left only one - the bedroom beside me. Raising my hand to silence my officers I turned the brass doorknob slowly and pushed the door only to find that it was locked. "Mr Worth," I called again. "We're arresting you in connection with the murder of Samuel Smith. You'll need to come with us. Open the door." Again, there was silence, only the sound of our breathing filled the passageway. I gave him a few moments to come to his senses, but as he didn't appear, I put my ear to the door, but there was no sign of movement in the room.

"Break down the door!" I ordered. The men steadied themselves but this time only one hard kick was needed, and we entered the room.

Asher Worth was sitting in his armchair facing the sea. His eyes were closed, and his cheeks were tear stained. I knew even before checking his pulse that he was dead.

THE CASE OF ASHER WORTH

Sixth Entry, 1939

As Asher Worth's body was being removed, one of my officers approached me.

"I found a note in his pocket, sir," he said, handing it to me. "It appears to be for his wife. He was clearly planning on doing a runner."

I took it from him and with a heavy heart opened it. It was written in fine handwriting:

By the time you read this I will be long gone. I apologise, my dear, for any undue stress the nature of my departure may cause. I cannot bear to live in this house for a moment longer with its memories. So, I am leaving but will always carry with me the burden of my guilt. Forgive me.
Asher

I passed the letter to another colleague who read it through and looked at me puzzled. "There's no mention of the murder, but he says he can't bear this guilt any longer. What guilt? Forgive him for what? The murder?"

I was just as puzzled as he was.

"What now, sir?"

"Now we wait for Mrs Worth to come home." I folded the note and put it in my pocket.

I was surprised when Jarvis suddenly appeared at the house. He strode in with a confidence that I had not seen in him previously and approached me.

"Can I have a word in private, sir? There's something that you'll want to know." We went into the dining room.

"What's so urgent?"

"The other day, when I was ill, and I went to the doctor, a lady came in, Mrs Evans. As we waited in the reception area, she happened to tell me that her son had recently died from a mysterious disease. She was extremely upset as they had been to London and paid a fortune for treatment which hadn't worked. She had since discovered that the same thing had happened to another family from this area."

I raised my eyebrows, not quite capturing where Jarvis was heading with this.

"Well, sir, that got me thinking and when I went into Dr Garth's office, he had to leave me for a few minutes because the receptionist wanted to speak to him, and I took advantage of his absence…"

"To do what?"

"To look for the Evan's file, and I made a very important discovery."

"That his cupboard was a mess?"

"Yes! No, I mean, sir, please…" he became flustered.

"Carry on, Jarvis, carry on!"

"I discovered that Dr Garth was receiving payment from a doctor in London for sending him clients for this treatment. The Worth file showed the same. There were letters confirming payment."

"Are you suggesting he was involved in a scam?"

"I am, sir. The doctor in London was giving treatments that did not work and receiving a huge sum of money for the privilege. And his friend, Dr Garth, was happy to provide him with those clients for a slice of the money."

I shook my head, hardly believing this turn of events. "So, there was no cure after all!"

"No, sir. It seems not. So, she would have died anyway."

I looked up sharply, "What do you mean, Jarvis? Who are you referring to? I thought the Evans child was a boy."

"Has nobody told you?"

"Told me what? I've just returned from London and came straight here."

Jarvis shook his head in disbelief, "I can't believe nobody has mentioned it, sir - Annie Worth died yesterday while you were away."

I sat down heavily on a chair. "And we've just found her father dead upstairs."

Now it was Jarvis' turn to look shocked. I handed him the note. He read it solemnly.

"Well, sir," he said at last handing it back to me, "whether he was guilty of involvement with the murder, or not, that poor man died believing it was his fault that he couldn't save his daughter."

I will never forget the look on Mrs Worth's face when she learnt of her husband's fate. She had suffered a double tragedy, made worse when she discovered the doctor's cruel betrayal of their confidence. By the time we went to arrest the doctor, he was long gone, leaving a very confused receptionist and an office full of destroyed papers.

As for The Magpie, he was charged with the murder of Samuel Smith as we had so much evidence against him. As Asher Worth was now dead, we closed the case quickly to avoid further scandal. Mr Ball was delighted that the money was returned to the bank's coffers and that no mention of its disappearance ever appeared in the press. The bank could continue its journey upwards.

Mrs Worth buried both her husband and daughter in the ancestral graveyard. She eventually remarried though and had another child whose name I cannot recall.

I moved on to new cases but never forgot Asher Worth because something about the case still bothered me. I thought I saw him once - striding along as he used to in his fine coat. He stopped, stared at me wordlessly and then carried on. When I turned around, he was gone. But sense tells me that it could not have been him.

It wasn't until I started to sort out my papers, ready to hand over before my retirement, that I came across the file again. My fingers lingered on the cover and then taking a deep breath I opened it. I shook my head, remembering The Magpie's evasive answers and that interminable train ride from London. I re-read his statement, which was as wordy and convoluted as his answers. One thing I did notice though, was one detail that Chief Constable Davies and I had overlooked on the night of the interview, being just a phrase among so many others and as tired as we were - 'dark-haired', but it now impacted me with the force of a blow, so much that I seemed to stop breathing. The night that The Magpie had met the man with the beard he had observed that the man was dark-haired and thus the colour of the man's beard was black. Black! Black! I wish I had realised this before because Asher Worth's beard was white!

And so it is that I finally closed the case of Asher Worth, although his memory will never leave me. May he rest in peace.

PART FOUR
- ASHER WORTH -

- XXXVI -

RENDEZVOUS
1982

Bentley wandered past the giant granite tower of Plymouth's iconic Guildhall, which stood like a proud Tuscan watchtower. He carried on toward the city's main church, the Minster Church of St. Andrew's, and then turned down a small road at the foot of its belfry. There was not much left of historic Plymouth after the Blitz, but the building he was headed for was a remarkable survivor.

Amongst the smoothed grey-granite buildings was a conspicuous white-washed hall. Yet despite its church-like appearance, it was a synagogue. The only dilemma now was to find the entrance, which wasn't where it was supposed to be on the main road.

Bentley scouted around and first impressions told him there was no entrance at all. The place seemed sealed up. He snooped about some more and then noticed a small door hidden inside the car park at the furthest point from the road. That must be it, he thought, there's nothing else. He walked up to it and knocked. There was silence inside. I've been stood up, he mumbled. Then he heard a jangling of keys and the door unlocked.

A slender lady of advanced years, but remarkably good health, greeted him. She was simply and elegantly dressed, her hair pulled back immaculately; it was jet black when it should have been silver. Her delicate porcelain complexion contrasted with her dark eyes.

"You must be Chester," she said with a soft smile, "Marina's waiting for you," and returned inside without waiting for confirmation. Bentley was left standing there with his hand in the air, waiting to shake hers. He stepped inside.

"You're late," scolded Marina. "I finished helping Mrs Nathan ages ago!"

"Yes, sorry about that, I couldn't find the door."

"It doesn't take a quarter of an hour to find the entrance."

"It almost did."

"It's really not difficult to find," laughed the lady.

"This is Mrs Nathan, the family friend that I told you about."

"I'm the caretaker of this *shul*," said Mrs Nathan. Bentley was confused.

"A *shul* is Hebrew for synagogue," explained Marina.

"Oh."

"The oldest operating Ashkenazi synagogue in the English-speaking world," added Mrs Nathan.

"Ashkenazi?" asked Bentley.

"You know," said Mrs Nathan, "the Diaspora here in Europe, we're European Jews."

Bentley nodded knowingly, not knowing what Diaspora meant. He looked up and around at the pristine white walls and the impressive stained-glass windows. Then he stared at the centrepiece.

"Ah, impressive isn't it?" sighed Mrs Nathan, noticing Bentley admiring it. "It's the only one of its kind in the UK. A Baroque Holy ark. Exquisite. Dutch made, then shipped over here. Beautiful. Never get tired of it."

The gold columns stretched high up to the encircling galleries above.

"What's inside it?" asked Bentley.

"The Torah scrolls," she said and saw Bentley's blank expression again. "Like the Old Testament scripts."

"It's amazing to think that this whole place survived the bombing of Plymouth, intact," said Marina.

"Ironic," said Bentley, "maybe Hitler's knew they were Ashkenazis."

"What do you mean?" said Mrs Nathan.

"You know, Ahke-*nazis*?" said Bentley, stressing the last word, happy with his humorous effort.

"Not the topic for making jokes, don't you think?" said Marina, wiping Bentley's smile clean from his face.

"No, no it's not. S-sorry."

"Ah, what are you being so ashamed about," interrupted Mrs Nathan. Bentley recovered his composure at once. "You're just a dumb kid," she continued, "it's no fault of your own. You don't know anything about these things."

Marina grinned.

"Can we go now?" a pale little boy appeared as if from nowhere and tugged at Mrs Nathan's arm. "I'm getting hungry."

"Yes, I'll be five minutes," she reassured him. "If you fetch my bag for me, then we'll be off. Marina's just leaving."

"Bye, Marina!" the little boy said shyly. "Thanks for reading to me."

"Bye, Alex," said Marina. "I'll see you next week."

"That's my grandson," said Mrs Nathan with a tear in her eye, watching as the child made his way to fetch her bag.

Marina placed a hand on her arm, "I hope things work out with Alex, Mrs Nathan," she said softly.

"I try to be optimistic, Marina but I just can't. The prognosis is not good. His poor parents will try and take him to Houston for the treatment if they can, but it may not be possible. It's so expensive you see."

"I'm very sorry to hear that, Mrs Nathan, really I am," Marina clasped the lady's hand tightly.

"Anyway, don't let me dullen your day with my sob stories," said Mrs Nathan. Marina kissed her on the cheek.

"Come on, Bentley," insisted Marina, "we should get going, or we'll be late to meet your friend."

"Friend?" asked a puzzled Bentley.

"Just come," said Marina.

"Okay you young ones. Have a nice time."

"It was nice meeting you Mrs..." suddenly, Bentley went dumb.

"Nathan," added Marina, but that was not what had made him stop talking.

"Are you all right, my dear?" asked Mrs Nathan.

Bentley remained silent a moment longer. No one else had noticed anything. He was the only one that could see the colourless outline of what seemed to be a man standing right behind Mrs Nathan. Why was there a ghost here? He thought. And why was it coming up toward him?

"Bentley?" said Marina. "Bentley!"

"Ye-yes, Nathan, you said. Sorry. I felt a bit wheezy." The image was still drifting toward him. Then it rushed at him like a gust of wind, turning him cold as it passed over him and it was gone.

Bentley suppressed a small helpless yelp.

"Well," said Marina, looking at him strangely, "you were saying that it was nice mee..."

"Meeting you," continued Bentley as he snapped out of his trance, "and it was."

"I'm glad to hear it. Same here, Chester. You seem such a polite boy."

"You have a beautiful *shul* here."

"Yes, I know, but it's nice of you to say so. I hope to see you again."

Outside, they headed toward the city centre.

"Can I ask you something?" said Bentley.

"Of course."

"If you could see that Mrs Nathan was upset, why did you have to upset her further by talking about her grandson. Why didn't you just let her be? Or at least try to reassure her or something?"

Marina stepped in front of Bentley to prevent him from taking another step, "Have you gone mad? You really think it would have been better to ignore her tears and pretend everything was all right? That's called indifference. I can't think of anything worse, can you?"

He could, but he suddenly felt very small.

"She needs to speak. People have to express their pain and you have to let them know they're not alone. I had no idea you were so unsympathetic towards other people's problems. Maybe it's because you're a boy and they don't tell you boys to express your pain, just suppress it." Marina was fuming. She finished her piece and stormed off.

Bentley looked as if his house had just been set on fire, and he had been the one that dropped the match. He stood there in silence, his innards twisted in all directions. He took a deep breath and decided to be brave. He ran after her and just caught up with her before she was about to cross the road where he would have lost her in the traffic. "Sorry, Marina!" he called out. She stopped but didn't turn round. "You're completely right. I-I don't know why I said that. I thought I was being nice, doing the right thing, by not prying, but… I'm glad you are angry with me, really. You *should* be angry with me. I'll try and be a better person from now on and think of other people's feelings in a different way."

"That's okay," she turned to address him. "You're the first boy that has ever said sorry for being stupid. Those kinds of situations are never easy. I also want to say thank you, for sticking up for me with Britton. I really feel as if it's my fault you got expelled."

"It's not your fault, it was all unintentional," he reassured her. "Now, do you mind if I ask you a different question?"

"Just as long as it is very different from the last one."

"What did you mean by a 'friend', back in the synagogue?"

"I thought we had met up to go and see this 'ghost' of yours."

"Oh, *that* friend," Bentley clicked. "Truthfully, I don't think we'll see anything, but I need you to help me crack the code."

"There's nothing Hebrew in it, is there?"

"Not yet, are you saying you don't understand Hebrew? But I thought all Jews read Hebrew."

"Whoever said I was Jewish?"

"You did – didn't you?"

"No, you did. And so did Britton."

Bentley stared at her for a moment and suddenly everything became clear. "So, you were serious the other day when you said that you weren't Jewish. I thought you were winding Britton up again with all that stuff about the origin of your name and everything."

"Well, if you think about it, Bentley, I *never* said I *was* Jewish. That was everyone else saying what they wanted to believe."

"But why did it never annoy you or anything?"

"Did you find anything annoying about Mrs Nathan?"

"No, she was charming."

"So, why would I feel offended by being compared to her. After all, as I've said before, she's a good friend of the family."

Bentley was flabbergasted. "You're amazing, Marina," he said, and suddenly felt a little embarrassed by the declaration, "But you'll be even more amazing if you help me crack that code," he added, trying to regain some composure.

"Let's go then!" said Marina. "The sooner we get this over with the better, I don't know why I'm letting you drag me into this."

"That's what friends are for," said Bentley, glancing at his watch. "Right, we should be able to get the next bus. The bus stop is just here."

"Who takes the bus when they can take a cab?" laughed Marina, raising a hand and waving, "Taxi!"

A black cab screeched to a halt and soon they were reclining in the sofa-like comfort of the back seat.

"So, what school do you think you'll go to, now that you can't get into Plymouth College?" asked Marina.

"I don't know. I think my parents are looking into alternatives. Anyway, I'd rather not think about that right now. We've still got the rest of the summer."

"Yeah, if we survive this spooky basement of yours," laughed Marina.

When the taxi stopped, Marina paid the fare and they entered Bentley's grand hallway.

"You kept this quiet!"

"It's home," Bentley said nonchalantly. "Do you want something to drink?" He led the way through the hall and out to the kitchen.

They went out to the garden to drink some ice-cream soda in the generous sunshine. Sherlock meanwhile yapped at the birds that had landed on the furthest trees and both Bentley and Marina had almost forgotten the point of their business.

The bliss was soon shattered as a violent breaking sound exploded from inside the kitchen.

"What was that?!" shrieked Marina. They both stood up and sped inside. Everything seemed fine in the kitchen, but then Bentley noticed a missing plate.

"Where is it?" asked Marina. They entered the adjoining dining room and found a mark gouged into the far wall.

"That wasn't there before," exclaimed Bentley. "Look here!"

Marina approached and saw the shattered fragments of the porcelain plate littering the floor in all directions. "Are you saying it flew across the room of its own free will?"

"I'm not saying anything. It seems perfectly obvious to me, despite how unbelievable it is to say it, but you witnessed it," said Bentley.

"I didn't see a thing. I only heard—"

"Exactly. You heard it. Now explain this: Sherlock is still out at the back of the garden, and we're the only ones here. Objects fall vertically, they don't fly horizontally unless otherwise propelled."

"It still doesn't mean it's true, I mean…" Marina pointed back at the kitchen but then saw something that stopped her from saying anything else. She stood in silent shock. Bentley joined her the moment he too saw what was happening. Another plate on the kitchen wall was wobbling, then the noise began to build as it rattled against the wall and then ripped off its fixings and flew across the open space. Marina and Bentley ducked and screamed as the plate whizzed between them, exploding into a storm of shattered pieces.

Marina cupped her hand over her mouth, "Oh, oh! I don't know what to say! I can't go into the cellar."

"We must," Bentley soothed his voice, despite the cold sweat that had just washed over him. "Listen, nothing will happen. I'll be there right next to you. Trust me. Nothing bad is going to happen." Marina looked at him disbelievingly. "It would have happened by now if it were," he added, and her panicked eyes relaxed, but only slightly.

"So, where is this basement?" she asked.

"Just through here."

"Gentlemen first."

RAIDERS OF THE LOST BOX
1982

"There's a door here, you say?" asked Marina, trembling slightly as they entered the dining room.

"Yes, there's a passageway behind there." Bentley pointed.

"A *secret* passage?"

"It's not really secret, you can see the door handle here."

"Oh, true, I didn't spot that," she admitted, a little embarrassed.

The door creaked open and Bentley switched the light on. It flashed on for a split second and then went out.

"That's not right," said Bentley, and flicked the switch back on but the bulb had blown.

"Has that ever happened before?"

"Never."

"I knew you were going to say that. Should we be doing this?"

"You're not scared, are you?"

"No. Are you? Your hair is sticking up," she looked at his tuft of hair sprouting up at the back and smiled nervously.

"Ha, ha," he said. "Now come on." He reached into the drawer behind her for candles and a box of matches. "Hold these." He bent down to remove the carpet tiles and lifted up the trapdoor. He grabbed hold of the chain once more and latched it onto the hook on the wall above. They both stared into the daunting black hole below them. Marina's eyes were wide open. "Marina? Marina!" called Bentley. "The candles?"

"Oh, yes. Here you go." Bentley struck a match and lit two of them, handing her one. He then started the descent and soon disappeared.

"Where are you going?!" hissed Marina.

"I thought you said you didn't want to come," replied Bentley, returning to look back up.

"I thought you said you would stay next to me. I don't want to be left up here on my own, especially with flying saucers."

"Technically, it was a plate. But sorry." He climbed back up a few steps and held out a hand to steady her as she came down. Step by step they slowly climbed down into the damp underground chamber. The candlelight cast dancing shadows onto the flaky white brickwork. The room beyond stood in sinister darkness. Bentley noticed Marina's heavy breathing and mutterings as she tried to calm her fears. He reached out his hand behind to hold hers and when she sensed it, she grasped it gratefully. Her tight grip almost squeezed the blood from his hand, but he smiled warmly to himself. Her presence calmed his nerves as well.

As they crossed the stone floor, the candle pushed back the shadows that had gathered in the far room. The main object came into view. Marina looked at the familiar candelabra, "Wow, it's a Menorah," she said. "Why didn't you tell me?"

"I didn't know what it was?"

"You might not know the name, but you must surely have realised that it was Jewish."

Bentley preferred to say nothing and plead ignorance, which was precisely the case.

"So, this is the meaning of the number seven you keep seeing."

"The candles in the chandeliers."

"You have candle-lit chandeliers?"

"It's not the luxury you think it is, especially when you're the one that has to take care of them."

"It has to be more than a coincidence."

"So, what do the candles mean?"

"The Menorah represents knowledge, where the six candles all incline slightly to the one in the centre."

"Oh, yeah," said Bentley, looking more closely. "They do lean in slightly." The Menorah glistened under the light and the effect made Bentley feel uneasy again, as if he had seen it somewhere before but he couldn't remember when or why.

"That is towards the light of the candle in the centre, which is God. And another symbolism is that the seven candles represent the seven days in the Old Testament for the creation of Heaven and Earth."

"You are a walking encyclopaedia. Wouldn't it be great if you could just type in a question like *'what is a Menorah?'* into one of those new computer things and then it would just give you the answer instantly, without having to go to a library and look it up in an encyclopaedia!" Bentley got excited at his idea.

"Can we focus on what we're doing here and stop dreaming things that are better off in sci-fi movies," Marina was clearly annoyed at the time wasting.

"Sorry, you're right," said Bentley.

"What about the inscription then around the border?" she asked, getting things back on track.

Bentley read it out again, "*A country without land, its kings and dignitaries are lifeless. If the king is annihilated, no one is left alive - 18,*" but Marina wasn't listening, she was studying the Menorah instead. "You said it was chess."

"And it is," she said.

"But I don't get it."

"That's because you didn't look here," she pointed at the square base, which the Menorah was resting on.

"I can't believe I didn't notice that before. It's a chessboard!"

"I'm not surprised, in this dim light. Now look at it more closely, do you notice anything strange about it?"

"There are letters on each of its squares and they are in alphabetical order."

215

"Are they?" she said leadingly. "Look closer."

Bentley did as he was told, excited that they were onto something and impressed that Marina understood exactly what was going on. "No, I don't see it," he replied, defeated.

"Are all the letters there?"

Bentley looked again.

"Yes."

"In the first 24 squares I admit they are all there, but in the other 40 squares where the alphabet is repeated until the end?"

"It's true some are missing!" he said in amazement. "The letters A, C, H and I."

"So, the missing letters must be relevant. What was the number in the riddle?"

"18."

"And if we rearrange the letters, they read the Hebrew word CHAI, which has a numerical value of—"

"18!"

"Precisely."

"And what does that mean?"

"I have no idea," Marina admitted abruptly.

"Really? No idea? You must have some."

"No. None at all."

"So, where do we go from here?"

"Can the box be opened?"

Bentley tried but it was a solid piece. "There's no lock, either."

"What if there were a latch? How would you unlock that?"

"With a combination number... the number 18!"

"Or in this case with a word in the correct order."

"That *must* be it!"

"I think so too," said Marina, really getting into the spirit of the mystery.

"What was the order again?" asked an eager Bentley.

"C-H-A-I," Marina spelt it out as she depressed each square in turn. There was nothing.

"Do it again," insisted Bentley.

"What difference will that make?"

"It hasn't been used for over a hundred years. Give it another go."

"If you insist," and she pressed the squares again, "but you're wasting your ti—" She stopped just as the box made a loud click. "I don't believe it!" she gasped.

"I do." Bentley lifted the lid and a musky smell wafted out. He held the candle nearer and there, under the dust, were a set of documents, an old map and a book. Carefully, Marina lifted them out, her eyes wide like the midnight owl.

"The documents are legal by the look of them," said Bentley, holding them closer to the candlelight.

"And this is a diary!" said Marina, opening it, "belonging to one Mr Asher Worth. Ever heard of him?"

"Never."

"Well let's find out who he is."

- XXXVIII -

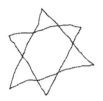

ASHER WORTH
1982

Bentley and Marina returned to the living room with the prized objects they had uncovered. Bentley was the first to sit down, "You can sit next to me," he said.

"What sort of seat is that?"

"A piano seat."

"It's big enough for two."

"That's the whole point."

"Never seen one used at the dinner table before."

"My mother loves it."

"That's so eccentric."

"So's the seat," smiled Bentley.

"I didn't mean your mother was—"

"Come on, sit down and read. Time is running out."

Marina joined him on the bench and together they opened the fragile diary. The crisp pages snapped apart. They held their breath, afraid the diary would fall to pieces and then the mystery would be lost forever.

They began reading the last entries where markers had been left at intervals, almost inviting them to follow their lead.

Asher Worth's Diary
1897
Today we moved into the house in Hartley Gardens. I stood on the doorstep with my wife - so proud to be able to provide this for our little family. The rooms are spacious,

and I can picture Annie running through them as she grows up. It is elegantly furnished - Dorothy has good taste and I can't deny her. I love to see little Annie's smile as she watches the twinkling dance of the chandeliers in the candlelight. It has fine views and I enjoy sitting in my chair upstairs and staring out to sea.

I have worked hard at the bank, often working overtime in my earnestness to further my career and to be able to provide everything that I desire for my family, as my family once did for me. I recently received a promotion and I was delighted, although there are some that say that I was not the first in line - however, I was chosen for a reason - my dedication and diligence.

"So, they had chandeliers, as well?" exclaimed Bentley.

"Everybody with a house like this had a chandelier back then," corrected Marina. "It's more surprising to have them now, not then. Let's keep reading."

"If we must."

"Do you want to get to the bottom of this mystery or not? It really looks like we're onto something."

"I suppose you're right, like always." Marina turned to the next page that had been marked.

1903
It was a fine day today. We spent it picnicking on Dartmoor. Dorothy made some challah bread in the morning - the smell of it filled the house but I was forbidden from stealing even a tiny piece. Annie helped to make it, interlacing the strips of dough with her little fingers. We tucked into it heartily on the moor and shook our crumbs for the birds to feast on. Little Annie does love it so. She runs around without a care in the world, playing hide and seek behind the huge lichen-covered rocks of Haytor, and as

light on her feet as the pixies that she eagerly searches for. She is such a happy child and laughs with delight at the ponies that roam freely, their tangled manes blowing in the wind. However, much as I love Dartmoor, there is something about the place, something dark despite the sunshine, an intangible undercurrent.

Today as we leant against the stones, she asked me to tell her the story about the treasure. When I asked her what story, she said, "The story that you told Mama about the family treasure! Sometimes I sit on the stairs and listen to you, you know." She's a little minx - the things she does and not yet eight years old! We'll have to be careful what we say. She begged me to tell her where the treasure is, but I told her only one thing - that the treasure is hidden and shall remain hidden in a safe place - where it has always been and where it will always belong. One day I will tell her the story though, after all, it does involve one of the most surprising artefacts in all England.

"What do you make of that, Bentley?"

"Unbelievable."

"But do you think this has anything to do with the ghost you say you've seen in the house?"

"It has to. What else could it be?"

"How can you be so sure?"

"I heard something up on the moor. A girl's voice on Haytor, remember?"

"Annie?"

"It must have been! It's too big a fluke."

"Oh, come on!"

"What was it Sherlock always says about the impossible?"

"Ah, I know the phrase," said a confident Marina, *"When you remove the impossible, whatever remains, no matter how improbable, must be the truth.* But a ghost is *impossible!* So, whatever it is that is *improbable* we just haven't stumbled across yet, I suppose."

Bentley stared at her. Even Marina wasn't sure she was right. She looked back at the diary to avert further disturbing thoughts.

"What does it say here?" she said, and the pair of them began reading again.

1904

It is with a heavy heart that I write my diary today. Little Annie has fallen desperately sick with a strange, seemingly incurable, illness. The doctor here says that he is unable to treat it. We are completely at its mercy. Our only hope is to travel with her to London where there is a doctor who is developing a new treatment, but the cost is far beyond our means. All our money has been sunk into the house. We are seeking a loan from the bank, despite there being another option available to us to secure the money and Dorothy and I have argued daily over it, but it is one that I fear I cannot rest much hope upon. Were I to try and sell the family heirloom, as my wife insists I must, we would not get but half the monies we require due to the recession that is gripping the economy, and there is no telling how long it would take to sell. But Dorothy is adamant that it is the right course of action. Meanwhile, I hold out for the bank to come through and support our cause. I can only pray that our precious Annie will recover.

~

It is just four months later, and my darling Annie is dead. We heard her restless and weak in the night and by morning her breathing was laboured. We fetched the doctor who told us that these were her final hours and all we could do, would be to keep her comfortable. She kept pointing to the window and saying something which I could not understand, but eventually she managed to whisper, The Moor - I want to go to the Moor.

My wife shook her head and said that we could not move her, could not take her out into the cold, but despite her protests and tears, I made preparations. The doctor, taking pity on us, offered us the use of his carriage and promised to accompany us. There were tears in his eyes and he could not fail to be moved by her plight.

I must admit that we drove the horses hard, the carriage shaking and jolting as we went. As Annie grew paler, the sky grew darker, as if in anger. We made the journey in excellent time. Annie's breathing was rasping, but as we approached our destination, she opened her eyes and smiled. We wrapped her in furs and then proceeded to walk to Haytor, the doctor following behind, his fine clothes blowing in the wind. Two ponies stood, watching our progress. Strangely enough, as we reached Haytor the wind died down and the sun peeked from behind a cloud as if wishing to witness this profound event, and receive her with the respect she deserved.

We sat in front of Annie's favourite rock. My wife sang softly, a gentle, soothing song. I held Annie in my arms. Her cheeks were tinged with colour from the cool air, it was the most colour I had seen in her face for a long time. She suddenly hugged me as tightly as she could and stared at the view until the colour in her cheeks faded and she breathed her last breath which was carried across the moor for all eternity.

My wife was inconsolable. She says that I am to blame - that I could have saved her but chose not to.

"That is some story," said Marina, wiping a tear from her eye.

"Yeah, it sure is, but we can't sit on this."

"Why not? It's a comfortable enough piano seat."

"Very funny. No, I mean we can't sit on this *information*. We have to go and find his grave right this minute."

"What? Go back to the synagogue and ask Mrs Nathan?"

"Why wait?"

"We haven't read all of the diary yet."

"Who needs to read *all* of this? We've learned all we need. Come on."

"No, *you* come on. We *have to* read till the end," insisted Marina, "We might have missed something."

"I think we've read enough. We know his name, his family, occupation and what happened to his little girl. What else is there to know?"

"We won't know unless we read *all* of it, will we?"

"Well, I have to lock up the house. So, you'll *have* to come."

"You'll see. You're just being brash and lazy," and Marina stormed past him.

They hurried out of the communal garden gates and waited at the bus stop.

"I don't know what let you persuade me to take a bus," Marina huffed.

"You act as if you've never been on one before."

"I haven't."

"Seriously?"

"Do I look as if I'm joking?"

"Never."

Marina frowned at his answer.

Bentley stepped into the street and hailed the approaching bus. Marina laughed.

"What?"

"Don't you think you're going a bit over the top?"

"They don't stop if they don't see you."

"Oh, in that case they've definitely seen you."

The bus began to slow down, and the doors swung open. Bentley looked up at the bus driver who stared back at him, but Bentley noticed something strange: his smile. But it wasn't a smile, it was a sardonic grin. Bentley followed the bus door as it skimmed alongside the pavement, but it didn't stop to let him plant his foot on the moving floor. The doors just closed, and the driver laughed as he drove off.

"That *never* happened!" cried Marina in sheer disbelief.

"It *definitely* happened."

"So, what do we do now?"

"There's only one thing, we can do."

"What's that?"

"Walk."

"Walk?!"

"Don't tell me it's the first time you've ever walked, as well."

Bentley paced on down the hill. "Don't worry," he said. Marina soon followed resentfully. "We'll take the next bus that comes along."

"Only if it stops!"

It wasn't long before the pair of them found themselves walking up to the synagogue door, but then Bentley saw something that made him freeze.

"What is it, Bentley?" asked Marina, noting his radical change.

"It can't be!" he pointed at a man with long dark hair entering the synagogue. The man turned round and when he set eyes on Bentley he was equally as surprised. He took off inside the building.

"You've come back!" came a startled Mrs Nathan, as Bentley rushed in.

"Did you see a man just come in here?"

"Can't say I did."

Then there came a noise out back. Bentley rushed over in its direction and found a chair positioned below an open window. Whoever it was they were well and truly gone.

"Are you all right, Bentley?" asked Mrs Nathan.

"I think I just saw my gardener."

"The house of God is open to all."

"That's not what I meant. But why would he come here?" he continued, speaking to himself, "he can't have been following me? I don't get the connection,"

"Why the problem with seeing your gardener? I thought you might be relieved to discover he's a man of faith."

"It's an odd story."

"It always is with you," said Marina, smiling. "I think you've got an overactive imagination. And if it was your gardener then maybe he's off to do someone else's garden."

"What? Out through the synagogue window?" Bentley frowned, unconvinced. "Anyway, we've come to ask you something, Mrs Nathan," he said, changing the subject. "Do you keep a register for the cemetery?"

"That's a strange request."

"It's an even *stranger* story," added Marina.

"Come," said Mrs Nathan, "the registers are kept here," and she pulled out a heavy ledger. "There are more here," she said, pointing at a row of identical documents, "if you need to go back further still."

"Thank you," said Marina.

"I'll leave you to it then. At my advanced age, the last thing I need to be looking at is a list of the deceased if you don't mind. Time for some tea I think."

Bentley and Marina watched her and then turned to hunt down the name of Asher Worth. They were bursting with the excitement of solving the mystery and finding the 'treasure' that had been mentioned in the diary. All thoughts of them following a ghost trail had left their minds entirely. They found 'W' but there was no Worth.

"It must be in another ledger," said Bentley.

"Yeah, this one was too recent."

They picked up another, it slammed down on the desk. Again, their hands raced to find the name of *Worth*, but there was nothing.

"It has to be in another," said Marina.

"It *has* to be." But another ledger soon came and went and then another and another, until the small section of records had been depleted and they were out of luck.

"It can't have been lost, can it?" said Bentley.

"We're missing something."

"If we've been guided to this point, then it hasn't been just to fail."

"For the moment I'm out of ideas," said Marina, "and now I really must get back home."

They thanked Mrs Nathan and left. Marina hailed a cab, while Bentley decided to walk back and take the time to think things over. He wandered through the grim seventies concrete back streets of the nightclub area before the green shady trees came down from the hill to greet him and usher him back home.

He entered the house and picked up the diary. Maybe I was too hasty in not reading everything after all, he thought. He slunk down into the Chesterfield sofa to read the remaining pages. It was the first time he had read something that wasn't for an exam.

He thumbed to the page they had been looking at. He was puzzled and flipped the page back and forth as if searching for a hidden trap door on the sheet of paper. It's only one more page, he thought. He felt stupid. I couldn't even be bothered to read one more page, he thought, and then I would have known the whole story. But then he felt worse when he realised that perhaps the vital clue he was looking for, wouldn't be contained in just one page of writing, despite it being the last one. Suddenly, he wished he had reams of material before him to read, so he could increase his chances of finding the missing evidence, but he didn't. Nervously, he began to read Asher Worth's last entry.

I am struggling to go on. I am wracked with guilt that I could have saved Annie but didn't. I do not understand why I did not do what I could to save her, for I could have sold the family treasure. But I was afraid of losing something that has been passed down for generations, something I should pass on to the next generation? But that generation is now gone, and the heirloom is of no use to my family. My foolish fear and pride let me hold on to something material instead of saving something precious. I put my faith and trust in God when I should have turned to the acts and reason of man to save her. If I could turn back time, I would do things differently. I have failed as a father and that to me is the lowest that a man can stoop. My daughter was my life - and now that she is no longer here, I have no life left. My wife looks at me with disgust in her eyes. I cannot return to the bank as if nothing happened, trudging backwards and forwards to earn a living for what purpose? For this living is no living now, when there is no one to create a home for?

Furthermore, the police appear to believe that I have something to do with Samuel Smith's murder as if I am a common crook and not the upstanding gentleman that I have always prided myself on being. I could never take another man's life.

Sometimes, I sit in my chair and stare out to sea, and my heart feels heavy. It even skips a beat or two. But my heart cannot break, can it, for it is already broken.

I have decided to go away, to give my wife a second chance at life. I do not know where I shall go, but I know that I will never find peace, not even on my deathbed or in the cemetery where I will one day lie with my ancestors. I will not be at peace until I make up for failing my Annie and my wife. My suitcase is packed but I leave my diary here, among other things so that they may one day lead to the salvation of my restless soul.

May my dear wife forgive me.

"But his ghost is here!" Bentley whispered as he finished reading the last entry. "He never left!" Then something began to unsettle his thinking, something annoying and deliberate. He looked up and saw the kettle was boiling. Who in the Devil's name switched that on? He turned round to see who it was, but he was the only one there. Then he twigged. He must be getting hotter in his search, he thought, the kettle had told him as much. He waited for a plate to fly off the wall, but he was spared the scene this time. The kettle was encouragement enough.

He jumped up off the sofa and phoned Marina.

"What is it, Bentley?"

"I've made a breakthrough!"

"That was fast. What is it?"

"I read the rest of the diary."

"I told you so!"

"Yeah, you were right. So, here it is: Asher Worth must have died here. And in his diary he mentions being buried beside his ancestors."

"You know what this means?" she said.

"Absolutely,"

"He's buried—

"Somewhere else," finished Marina.

"Exactly!"

"But where?"

"I haven't figured that out yet," admitted Bentley.

"We'll have to go back ask Mrs Nathan."

"Poor Mrs Nathan she's going to be sick of seeing us. But before we do that, I have to go back up to the bedroom."

"Why?"

"I think that's where Asher Worth died. There's something I have to find out."

"Are you crazy?! Don't do it! It's way too dangerous, you'll—"

"Marina? Marina?!" The line had gone dead.

Then came a loud crash from upstairs as the bedroom door slammed shut. The noise rang out like a gun shot through the large house. It made Bentley jump, but it didn't scare him half as much as what came next.

At first, he wasn't sure if his mind was playing tricks on him but then he heard it again, only this time louder. It was a muffled voice from inside the room.

"*Bentley… Bentley… come,*" it called out to him.

- XXXIX -

TERROR
1982

Bentley replaced the phone receiver and slowly forced himself to walk to the bottom of the staircase. He had been here before, nervous and hesitant, but nothing had happened on the previous occasion. This time though he was worried, he could sense the air was different. He sensed something different was going to happen, and he suspected he wasn't going to enjoy it. His hands were damp with sweat and his heart felt fragile as it pounded against his chest.

The sound Bentley had been waiting for from upstairs began. He took his first step towards his dark destiny.

His legs trembled; his muscles feather-light with anxious energy, but he managed to reach the landing. He crept up the final flight of stairs, his hand gripping the banister fiercely, white with tension. As he arrived at the top of the stairs, he saw the master bedroom door creak open as if expecting him. And it was.

For a moment a wave of pathetic panic seized him. Then he strengthened his resolve and broke through the fear that was sensibly trying to hold him back. Despite his weakness, he would not turn and leave until he passed through the door. He mumbled to himself, "He's a friendly ghost, friendly ghost... friendly. Nothing bad will happen. Nothing. Just go in and... face it. The ghost has brought you here. Come on, Bentley! You can do this!"

He stood in the doorway and there, slumped in the armchair, almost without warning and looking out to the distant sea, was the grey, translucent being. The elegant gent sat in his Edwardian morning suit, his head buried in his hands, sobbing deeply. Bentley's eyes flared open in horror and excitement. He had to steady himself momentarily, the blood-rush to his head made him feel uneasy. The crying began to decrease and gradually the man stopped his grief-stricken weeping and all signs of movement. Bentley had just witnessed the moment of Asher Worth's death and now dared to venture nearer.

For a moment, Bentley was unable to breathe as his eyes fell upon the grotesque scene of the dead man in the chair. But how had he died? Had he been poisoned? It seemed as if he had just cried himself to death.

The gentleman's neat hair was ruffled and the eyes... Bentley couldn't see the eyes. He stepped closer, almost expecting to hear something. Then he saw what he thought were his eyes: empty dark disks. He wished he had Marina's support. She made him feel brave. And then he heard something, it was faint at first but as he neared the ghostly figure, he realised it was directed at him. He squinted as he attempted to hear the faint voice, which emanated from the mouth of the eerie corpse.

"Saaaa hiiii," he heard and stepped closer.

"*Save him*," the ghost heaved.

"S-save who?" Bentley dared ask.

"*Save him*," repeated the ghost sternly.

"But I don't know who you mean," he managed to say.

The ghost lifted its head in anger, its dark eyes now trained on him. Bentley stepped backwards.

"Save him!" it screamed, and dissolved into thin air.

Bentley slowly regained his normal breathing, after the outburst had knocked the wind out of him and returned downstairs. He headed straight for the kitchen sink, but as he turned into the living room next to the kitchen, he was at once seized by the arms by an intense force. The shock and pain knocked the wind from his lungs. His eyes were agape with wild panic as he looked into the crazed gaze of the gardener who had grabbed him and forced him up against the wall.

"What is it?! What is it?! I must know!" he wheezed in a gruff voice, covering Bentley's face and clothes with spittle. Bentley fought to breathe and tried to imagine what the lunatic meant.

"The ghost?"

"Yes, yes, you've seen it too! What does it want from us?"

"Us?" Bentley was turning red, his body was being crushed.

"I was here first! You have no idea of the hours I've spent trying to understand what it wants."

"You came into the house that night?"

"Just tell me!" the man pulled out an object and pressed it into Bentley's gut, "or I'll—"

He never finished the sentence. The police sirens saw to that. As soon as the man heard them, he was gone as quickly as he had appeared.

Bentley heard the keys jangle in the front door and then the police came in, accompanied by Bentley's parents.

"You all right son?" said his father. "I told you the police were onto it. Turns out, the gardener was no gardener. I can't believe I fell for those false references."

"That's why the petunias have been dying!" exclaimed Bentley's mother.

"He did know the previous owners though. He was their nephew. Seems he made a copy of our back-door key. But what he wanted with this place, who knows? All he kept screaming was, 'It's hidden in this house!' Bonkers, if you ask me."

Bentley left his parents to deliberate. He took a seat to get a grip on his thoughts, and when he had finally gained some colour in his cheeks, he phoned Marina.

"Bentley! You're all right! Thank God," she said gleefully.

"Thank the police, more like. Can you meet me at the synagogue on Saturday? Say around ten?"

"You can count on it."

"Great, I have to go now," and without waiting to hear her reply, his trembling hand replaced the receiver.

"Ghosts!" he said. "I hope that's the last time I ever see one."

- XL -

THE OLD JEWISH CEMETERY
1982

Bentley stood under the gaze of St. Andrew's Gothic bell tower, the pristine red and white flag of St. George fluttering in the sea breeze that was coming up from The Sound.

"Sorry, I'm late," puffed Marina as she arrived. "Have you been waiting long?"

"Not as long as Asher Worth."

"You really think he's trying to lead you to something in the cemetery, don't you?"

"There's only one way to find out."

"Let's begin the treasure hunt then."

They carried on down Catherine Street to the synagogue to speak with Mrs Nathan, one last time.

"What makes you think it's treasure?" asked Bentley in a suspicious tone.

"I don't, it was just a figure of speech. Stop getting so nervous and jumping to conclusions."

"If you had seen the things I have seen, you'd be the same, believe me."

"You going to tell me what you saw now?"

"It's better I don't."

"But you distinctly heard a voice say, 'Save him'?"

"No question."

"But save who? He had a daughter not a son, and he can't be referring to himself either."

235

"A lot of strange things have happened, which I would find hard to believe if I hadn't seen them myself."

"That's why I think I believe you, but I'd rather it wasn't true."

"Really? Doesn't a 'good' ghost story normally liven things up?"

"Or quieten things down, if it's a scary one."

They reached the door and found Mrs Nathan outside, tending a few of the flowers.

"Why, what a surprise! I really didn't think I'd see you two again so soon."

"We have something to ask you," said Marina.

"By all means."

"Can we ask you inside?"

"Sounds mysterious," said Mrs Nathan, smiling like a naughty child.

"It is," replied Marina.

They entered the synagogue and found a place to sit.

"What is all this cloak and dagger business about then?"

"We need to locate someone, and you just might be able to help us," explained Marina.

"I have the phone register of our congregation here."

"I don't think you'll be able to contact them that way," said Marina.

"Is there *another* Jewish cemetery?" asked Bentley.

Mrs Nathan laughed, "No, I'm afraid not, the Jewish community is not that large."

The phone rang, "You'll have to excuse me for a moment," and she scuttled off to answer it.

Bentley took out the map he had found amongst the documents from the basement and studied it carefully.

"He must have been buried with his ancestors, somewhere else," said Marina.

"We'll have to think of something different then," said Bentley. He continued staring down at the map, "Doesn't it look to you as if the cemetery is in a different place?" Marina leaned to look for herself.

"I can't tell where anything is on this map," she said, "it's so old and faded."

"Maybe you're right, it just seems to be in a weird place. Aren't there houses here?"

"It's such a small historic area, everything has been built over. They say it's the largest cobbled area in England. So, there can't be a vacant green plot of that size here."

Mrs Nathan returned.

"Are you all right?" Marina asked. "You look as if you have just received shocking news."

"I have. All these years… and I never knew."

"Never knew what?" asked Marina.

"A gentleman just phoned to complain about branches from the cemetery, affecting his telephone line."

"Is that true?" asked Bentley.

"Well, no. The cemetery has just been cleared of overgrowth, but he insisted."

"Did you ask where he was?" said Marina.

"He said Lambhay Hill, up on The Hoe seafront."

"Is there a cemetery there?" asked Bentley, whose voice was growing with excitement.

"It's impossible," said Mrs Nathan. "If there was, I would know, wouldn't I? We all would know. You can't just hide or forget something like that."

"However, if there is a forgotten, walled-up cemetery there," said Bentley, "then the key has to be somewhere in the synagogue."

Mrs Nathan's eyes lit up at the suggestion, and she lifted out a dusty box, brimming with a mangled mesh of old rusty keys. "If I have the key to the door, then it will be in this very box," she said.

Bentley peered into it and began to rummage around.

"You have a lot of keys," said Marina.

"It's this one!" said Bentley at once, plucking out a lone key.

"Don't be ridiculous," Marina laughed, "How could you possibly guess that?"

"It's hot."

"It never is!" exclaimed Mrs Nathan and took the key out of his hand. She dropped it at once, letting it fall back amongst the others.

"My word! It *is* hot!" she shrieked disbelievingly.

"Let me see that," said Marina and fished it out. "That can't be!" she said, as she felt the inexplicable warmth of the object, passing it from hand to hand.

"Let's go and unlock that door," said Bentley. "We've got a twenty-minute walk ahead of us."

"We could always take a—"

"No," Bentley interrupted her.

They walked out to the main road and followed it down to the entrance to Southside Street that meandered through the heart of Plymouth's historic harbour. The area was now given over to pubs, the famous gin distillery, shops selling trinkets and artists peddling wares. The smell of stale beer and fish and chips filled the air, while seagulls played their incessant din above them.

They found the hill in question, leading up behind the cobbled streets and up past the imposing Citadel fort.

"It should be just about here," said Bentley.

"I don't see anything here," replied Marina

"You know what? Neither do I."

"If it's been hidden all these years, that's what you should expect."

The adventurous pair paced up and down the area, retracing their steps several times.

Marina started to flap her arms, visibly irritated and losing her patience.

"Hang on, what's this behind here?" exclaimed Bentley.

Marina ran down the road to join him. They pushed past a tree and entered a small area that looked like private property.

"What do you think?" he said, pointing at a weather-beaten dark blue door.

"This *has* to be it!" squealed Marina.

They approached the ordinary-looking door set into a large speckled granite wall. Bentley reached out the key. With a trembling hand he inserted it into the lock. It fitted. He turned it. Nothing happened, but the key got jammed. He tried harder to turn it.

"Be careful you don't break it!" said Marina. But then there came an almighty crack. He stopped for a moment, worried that he had, indeed, broken it. He turned the key one final quarter rotation and it ended with a delicate click. Marina gently pushed against the old door and it slowly glided opened.

Inside was a green wonderland; a lush seascape of waves of foliage that rolled from wall to wall.

"Would you believe that!" exclaimed Bentley. He ducked under the vegetation and there under the green tent were gravestones.

"A real hidden cemetery! But is it Jewish?"

Bentley moved closer to reveal a tombstone with Hebrew inscriptions on it. Marina followed Bentley, "This is definitely it, all right!" she squealed.

"How will we find the grave we are after?"

"It's a bit scientific but I think we should look for the one that says 'Asher Worth' on it."

"True... good, research professor," said an embarrassed Bentley.

"Let's get to work then. You go off in that direction and I'll go straight ahead."

With squawking seagulls circling above the two intrepid hunters, they forged their way through the interwoven branches. It did not take long for them to flounder, fighting against such stubborn overgrowth.

"Any luck?" called out Marina from the far wall, breathing heavily and wiping the sweat from her forehead.

"Not yet, I can't even read some of these headstones, they're so worn!"

They continued hacking their way through the brambles and snapping branches. When Bentley reached the last gravestone at the end of his row, he removed the plant covering and cried, "Bingo!" Marina waded over to share in his discovery.

"Well?" she said. "Does it say Asher Worth?"

"No."

"What?! You made me come all the way over here for—"

"But I think I've found what we're looking for," Bentley lifted the curtain of dangling branches and leaves to reveal a large rectangular tomb, different to all the rest, and big enough for a body to be laid to rest in. It was ancient-looking and possessed no writing, only a solitary image on the top, which had faded. The image of two slanted lines, however, was just clear enough so one could understand its purpose.

"Horns?" said Marina. "What has that got to do with Asher Worth?"

"I don't know but this tombstone must be the one. There is nothing else on the other tombs and the horns— well, the horns *are* relevant," replied Bentley. "You remember the library? They're a symbol for Moses."

"There's only one way then to find out if that's what they mean here," said Marina, "and that is—"

"Open the tomb."

"Where do we start though?"

Bentley cleared the rest of the plants from around the tomb and looked for a way to open the lid on the large tomb, but he found nothing.

"What about this?" asked Marina, who was wiping dirt away from the front of the tomb. She revealed the following shapes:

"Okay, what does this represent?" asked a baffled Marina.

"You really don't know? I thought it was obvious."

"Why else would I be asking?"

"They're the different parts of the Chai symbol, aren't they?"

"Oh, yeah. But I still don't get what they have to do with anything."

"I suppose they are the key." Without wasting a second more Bentley started applying pressure on the different shapes until one of them jumped and slid across the stone surface.

"Wow!" yelped Marina with delight.

Bentley then moved to another shape until he arrived on the piece that would move next. He had to try hard to get the pieces to budge, pieces that had spent many years exposed to the damp. But one by one they eventually yielded, jumping into life and sliding into their allotted place, until a familiar symbol came into view:

"Bentley, you're a genius!"

"Don't say that too loud, or Troswell might hear you."

"To hell with Troswell! He wouldn't know a good idea if it came up to him. And to think you failed the Eleven Plus."

She was silent for a moment, wishing she hadn't just mentioned him failing exams. "So, to open it," she continued, "I suppose you just press it." She leaned forward and pressed the newly-formed Chai symbol. Nothing happened. She tried harder, but still no luck. She had a further attempt on each individual section of the Hebrew character, but again it was futile.

Then Bentley raised his hands on the rim of the tomb's covering and with barely any effort at all, lifted the lid. Marina's face went blank.

"How on Earth did you know that was the way to do it?"

"I didn't, but as you had tried every other possible way, it made sense that this was the only *probable* method left. That, of course, and the fact that I heard it click open."

Marina shoved him playfully.

"Are you ready for this?" Bentley asked in a climactic voice.

"Don't get your hopes up, Bentley, this is not some adventure novel."

"I know, but it feels like it, doesn't it?"

"Come on, let's get this anti-climax over with."

Bentley opened the lid fully and they could see a complex lever system which made easy work of lifting such a heavy object. Their eyes opened in wonder when they saw what was hidden inside. In the centre of the solid stone top was a small recess and, in its centre, a black metal box which filled the cavity perfectly.

Together they lifted out the box. On its lid was the coat of arms Bentley recognised, the symbol his father had so strangely drawn in the woods and the one also in his school textbook. The shield contained a wavy line and above and below it a star, representing the northern and southern hemispheres. It was Drake's coat of arms.

They eased open the box.

"The contents are perfectly preserved," said Marina in astonishment. "How did they do that?"

"Completely sealed from water or anything else."

"Unbelievable."

Marina pulled out a parchment with elaborate handwriting on it. "Look at this!" she said in a hushed, reverent voice.

"What is it?"

"A letter. But it's no ordinary letter." And she read it out:

Moses,
'To the greatest navigator there e'er was and an even greater friend.'
     Sir Francis Drake

"You can't be serious, *the* Sir Francis Drake?" gasped Bentley.

"So, the Moses we've been looking for was his navigator? Not the one from the old Testament?"

"We still don't know why we have been contacted from beyond the grave."

"What else is in here?"

Bentley unfolded the cloth that was wrapped around the contents of the box, revealing a shining mass of metals.

"Are those gold coins?" said Marina.

Bentley picked up one, "Spanish pieces of eight," he said.

"How do you know that?" Marina was impressed.

"My old man collects coins, and this is the only one I ever remember."

"So, we've found treasure!"

"Armada treasure it seems. But wait… what's this? There's something else under here."

"Really? There's more?"

Bentley lifted out the four objects that had caught his attention.

"Are you all right, Bentley?" Marina could now see what he had in his hands. "Wooden balls?"

"You don't know what you're looking at, do you?" he lifted one closer and twisted it round.

"What's that?"

"A silver stamp."

"Yes, but read the inscription."

"Sir Francis D."

"Are you telling me that these are the—"

"The very ones."

"No. It's impossible! They're more valuable than the coins."

"Immensely more! These four objects are the real treasure."

"You know your name is going to be all over the papers for this."

"I hope not," said Bentley.

"You've got no choice. And what's this inscription here on this one: '*I did not finish me game but I did thrash the Spaniards.*'"

"Oh my God! This is even more unbelievable. I thought the finding of the hidden cemetery was enough, but this… this is huge!" declared Bentley.

"What is England going to say when they discover that a schoolboy has just unearthed Sir Francis Drake's *boules*. They *are* his bowls, aren't they?"

"They have to be. An expert will have to be the judge though. But look at this one, it has a deep gash in the side. No idea what happened to that one. Looks like someone slashed it with something," said Marina.

"I think I'm going to faint."

"Don't do that, Bentley, I'll never be able to carry you out."

"Come on then. Let's get back and tell Mrs Nathan the incredible news."

"What do you mean 'tell Mrs Nathan'? We have to tell the world!" she exclaimed dramatically. "You're going to be famous Bentley!"

"Not again!"

- XLI -

A TALE OF THE UNEXPECTED
1982

They locked the old door to the secret cemetery behind them as Bentley cradled the box under his arm and began their excited walk back to the synagogue.

"You know," said Marina, "you'll have to get your parents to come and pick you up after speaking with Mrs Nathan."

"Why do you say that?"

"You can't go round Plymouth with a national treasure under your arm as if it were some West Country souvenir tea towel."

"Good point. But I don't have any tea towels."

"That's not my point."

"I know, just joking, but I'll be happier when this thing is safe inside."

When they arrived back at the synagogue, Mrs Nathan was there expecting them. "Any luck you two detectives?"

"You won't *believe* our luck!!"

"Really? I am surprised. What did you find?"

"A hidden cemetery!" exclaimed Bentley.

"*Beit almin?*" asked Mrs Nathan in Hebrew.

"Yes, it's a Jewish cemetery," replied Marina.

"That is astonishing! I have to let the community know."

"And the press," said Marina.

"But whatever led you two there?"

"It's a long story, Mrs Nathan," answered Bentley.

"Bentley thinks he saw a ghost."

"I don't follow," said Mrs Nathan.

"He lives in this big fancy house in Hartley Gardens and thinks some spirit was contacting him."

"There is *definitely* something in the house," said Bentley. "If not, you try and explain the Menorah in the cellar and the riddle that led us here."

"Wait a minute," gasped Mrs Nathan, "you say you live in Hartley Gardens?" she was beginning to tremble.

"Are you all right, Mrs Nathan," asked Marina, concerned for the old lady.

"I don't know, it depends on what Bentley says next. Do you know the name of this ghost that has, as you say, *contacted* you?"

"Yes."

Mrs Nathan stumbled back a step.

"His name is Asher…"

"*Worth*," said Mrs Nathan, breathing new life into the word and then she collapsed unconscious on the floor.

"Mrs Nathan? Mrs Nathan? Can you hear me? Mrs Nathan?" called out Marina, as Bentley dabbed a wet cloth on the lady's forehead. Mrs Nathan lay with her head in Marina's arms. They heard a slight groaning and then the elderly caretaker began to move before she eventually opened her eyes. She looked up at the two youngsters peering down at her and she smiled.

"I am sorry," she said. "I didn't mean to faint. But it has been so many years since I last heard the name of Asher Worth - poor Asher."

"You *knew* him?" asked an incredulous Marina as she helped her to her feet. She pulled up a seat for her and sat down alongside.

"Uncle Asher, as he was known in the family."

"So, he was your uncle!" said an amazed Bentley. "That's incredible!"

"Not *quite* my uncle. But don't forget, Plymouth is a relatively small world. Such coincidences are bound to occur more than you expect."

"Tell us the story of how you and Asher Worth are connected," Marina pleaded.

Bentley's attention was suddenly taken by something moving towards them. A transparent, silvery figure came and sat quietly behind Mrs Nathan, adjusting his monocle. Neither of the ladies could see the gentleman stroking his beard as if waiting for his story to be told.

"It's not a happy one I'm afraid, but life is like that for a good many people - too many in fact. You two are very young, but it is one of life's lessons, I'm afraid. We may surround ourselves with beautiful things but there can be no protecting us from the cruel indifference of life itself."

Mrs Nathan smiled calmly and prepared herself for the tale.

"Asher Worth's family has a long and distinguished history, albeit a silent one. He is descended from the Jewish navigator Moses, who circumnavigated the globe with Drake, and later fought alongside him against the Armada. But our story begins with Asher at the turn of the century, when he married my mother, Dorothy. They were happy together and doing well, hence the house Bentley now lives in. But sadly, it was not to last long. Their daughter, Annie, fell ill and needed treatment, but it was costly. There was talk of a family heirloom that they should have sold but Asher, apparently, so the story goes, did not want to lose it and so the girl never received the treatment in time and perished.

The poor man died, it seems, of a broken heart. But then, who wouldn't? It took my mother a long time to even begin to get over her double calamity, but eventually she remarried, and I was their first child. Although she never talked of the daughter she lost, everyone in the family knew of the tragedy and the fate that had befallen Asher. That was way back in 1904. Times have changed so much, but such tragedies will continue to occur, and in the same fashion. Progress will never change that."

"That is quite some story," said Marina.

"Yes, it is," agreed Bentley, who then saw the ghostly man place a caring hand on Mrs Nathan's shoulder.

"It's a bit cold in here all of a sudden, isn't it?" said Mrs Nathan. "Or is that just me?"

- XLII -

ANOTHER DOOR
1982

The happy times for Bentley, however, seemed to have come to an abrupt end when he was called into the living room to speak with his parents.

"Ah, there you are my dear," said his mother. "What with all the excitement of late and the possibility of you discovering something - dare I say it, of national importance, we haven't been able to talk." She then flashed a glance at her husband.

"Errm, that's right, son. Please sit down. In light of your recent academic difficulties—"

"You mean my failing the entrance exam into Plymouth College?"

"That's the one, took the words right out my mouth. That and the nasty business with that bully Britton."

"How is he doing?" asked Bentley.

"Oh, he'll pull through all right. You youngsters always do. Anyway, the point is that your mother and I—"

"Your father and I have come to the decision," said his mother interrupting as she would often do when she asked her father to speak for both of them, "that the best step forward would be going to Buckland House."

"Where?" Bentley knew most of the schools in the area but had never heard of Buckland House.

"It's a boarding school, son," clarified his father.

"A *boarding* school?" Bentley felt as if he had been punched in the gut.

"Now, there's no need to go getting all melodramatic, Chester dear," his mother said. "It's a marvellous place with rugby, swimming, billiards and they even have shooting. You'll have a splendid time of it and won't even want to come home, will he dear?"

"No, no, quite. Now, it really is the best option, son. If you want to go to Plymouth College eventually, then this will give you another shot at it. What do you say?"

Bentley's head was spinning. Everyone knew that only badly-behaved children went to boarding school.

"Now, don't go thinking that this is where they send bad children because it is nothing of the sort," said his mother, reading his thoughts.

"*Au contraire*," added his father. "It's a beautiful place my boy, and you'll have a great time of it. Wish I'd gone myself."

His father was right, but Bentley couldn't see it that way.

"All right then," Bentley finally rescinded. "If you are sure it is the best."

"We are son."

"There we are!" squealed his mother. "Not difficult after all," and she duly clinked her sherry glass with her husband's. "Besides, who knows what adventures you'll have there!"

Suddenly, her glass fell from her hand, smashing in all directions as it impacted the side table. Bentley went rigid. His parents were moving about and speaking to him but he could not hear them. He was somewhere else. He heard the sound of further breaking glass and a muffled scream. He felt frightened but didn't know why. He wanted to enter the door he saw in front of him and see what had broken the glass. He lifted his hand to pull the door back and just as he was about to do it he felt someone grabbing his hand and something wet.

"There you go Chester," said his mother snapping him out his daze, "you can help your father mop up. I'll fix myself another sherry."

"Are you just going to stand there, son?"

"N-no," and he started to slowly clean the side table but his thoughts were clearly elsewhere. What was this house he kept seeing? Was it really him there or someone else? Was it something to do with when he was little or was he going mad now he had seen a ghost? He had more questions than answers.

YIZKOR
1982

It was another fine day for tending roses and Bentley's nan was busying herself by pruning and singing to her favourite floral creations. Bentley sipped cold lemonade, while waiting for the phone to ring, but before it did, he had one last thing on his mind.

"Nan, why do you think ghosts exist?"

"Oh, I wouldn't go round asking questions like that my dear, people will think you're barking mad."

"Is that why there are more ghost sightings in the UK than anywhere else?"

"I hadn't thought of it like that, but you've got a point there my dear," she chuckled to herself. "No, I suppose if such things exist then spirits are simply troubled souls that left a life's work undone, they are left searching for some way to reconcile the past. You could call it purgatory, I suppose."

"And what happens when they reverse the situation?"

"Complete what they had left undone? For that to happen they would have to provoke things to happen, make people do things I suppose, to make up for their wrongdoing in the past. Why do you say that exactly?"

"Nothing, I was just curious."

The phone rang.

"I'll get it," said Bentley.

"It's for you anyway," she said but he didn't hear her.

Moments later, he came rushing back out into the sunshine.

253

"Nan! Nan! It's real! It's real!"

"Your find, you mean?"

"It's been authenticated. They are the bowls of Sir Francis Drake!"

"Looks like your life is about to change young Chester. The phone will be falling off the hook soon with people wanting to talk to you."

"Really? I don't want to talk to anyone right now. I have some other business to do."

"*Business*, you say?" and she laughed at his adult manner. "Where are you off to now in such a hurry?" she called out after him.

"Sorry, Nan, I have to rush into town, there's someone I have to meet."

"Well, you go and have a good time, but be careful out there."

"I will. Love you, Nan."

"Love you too, Chester."

As soon as the door closed behind him, the phone rang again. His nan answered it, "The Plymouth Herald you say? No, he's not here. No, I have no idea where he could be."

She put the receiver down, "Oh Chester," she said. "I told you to be careful about using your gift."

Bentley walked up onto The Hoe promenade. Out before him was the bay of Plymouth Sound filled with pleasure craft making the most of the bright sunshine and fair wind. He carried on to the white and green pavilion that sheltered benches and afforded them a panoramic view out to sea.

Sat together were Mrs Nathan and Marina, admiring the splendid scene and in front of them was a sprinkling of green and white striped deck chairs. The wind bloated their canvas material fully out and then let it fall back into place again. Bentley watched the choreography of the chairs being played like wind instruments, but just as he was about to join the others, he saw the most curious thing. The deck chair closest to Mrs Nathan and Marina, suddenly went taut as if someone had just sat in it, and yet there was no one there.

"Congratulations," said Mrs Nathan as she saw Bentley arrive. Marina was beaming from ear to ear.

"Whatever for?" he said.

"Why, the bowls of Sir Francis Drake, of course. They've been authenticated, haven't they?"

"It's all over the news," said Marina.

"Wow! News really does travel fast. Or at least faster than the bus service that got me here."

"So, why did you call us here, Bentley?" asked Marina. "As if we didn't have better things to do with our time rather than obey your commands."

"Yes, I'm sorry for the hassle but once you hear what I have to say, I am sure you will both agree that this was arguably the best place either of you could be in the world right now."

"In the *world?*" said Marina. "That's quite some claim."

"And this is quite some moment you are about to witness. Trust me."

"Mrs Nathan, you're related to Asher Worth, indirectly, aren't you?"

"Yes, I suppose one could say that."

"And I now know why I was led to this treasure and why Asher Worth, specifically, contacted me to find it."

"You know why?" asked an amazed Marina.

"Yes, I do. It took me some time to work it out, but I believe the objects are for you, Mrs Nathan. Not for me."

"Whatever for?"

"Asher Worth lost his daughter and didn't react in time. He should have sold the family heirloom to pay for her treatment. But for some reason, now lost in time, he didn't do that. This here," he produced the box containing the bowls and gold coins, "is that very heirloom. You are its natural and legal benefactor."

Mrs Nathan began to cry, incapable of words. Marina was also starting to get emotional.

"So, we know what this treasure, if you want to call it that, is meant for," continued Bentley.

"Oh, Bentley," said Marina, "this is too much," tears were welling in her eyes.

"Asher Worth wants you to have this, to do what he failed to do, and in this case, it is meant to pay for your grandson's treatment in— where was it?"

"Houston," replied Mrs Nathan.

"Exactly. This is who Asher Worth wants us to save."

"But the government will take this as a national treasure, won't they?" added Marina.

"The bowls maybe, but not the coins, and they will still pay for the bowls, but just stop you from selling it to a third party for a higher sum. That's what my father says anyway."

Mrs Nathan stood up and hugged Bentley.

"I really don't know what to say."

"I do," he replied.

"You do?" said Marina.

"Yeah, who wants an ice-cream?"

"Really?" said Mrs Nathan. "That's your price?"

"I drive a hard bargain, I know."

"That's some expensive ice-cream," said Mrs Nathan joyfully.

"Exactly, it's West Country vanilla ice-cream, after all."

"You look after the box," said Mrs Nathan, "and I'll be back with the payment."

She wiped the tears from her eyes and headed to the ice-cream van parked up behind them.

"That was amazing, Bentley," said Marina as she watched the happy lady leave.

"I told you it would be worth your time."

"That's an understatement if there ever was one. Listen, there's only one thing I still haven't understood about this whole story."

"Which is?"

"Why were the bowls we found classified as *bar* bowls by the experts? What's the relevance of that?"

"It's just as Mr Pendrift said in class."

"What do you mean?"

"He mentioned an alternative version to the famous story of Drake playing bowls up on The Hoe."

"Which was what again?"

"That he wasn't on The Hoe, he was in a local tavern when the message of the Armada reached him. He was playing bar *boules*."

"That's what these skittles are!" she looked inside the box and picked one of them out.

"It lends credibility to the story, I suppose."

"It wouldn't do to have a captain of the fleet drinking at a time of pending war."

"It did sound like a drunken boast, didn't it? Saying he would finish his game and thrash the Spaniards."

"That's why there was 'plenty of time'," realised Marina.

"It wasn't just because the tide was not favourable for them to sail out, but Drake needed to—"

"Sober up!"

"Exactly," said Bentley.

Mrs Nathan returned and handed out the ice-cream. Bentley indulged himself, taking in the last of the summer sunshine.

Mrs Nathan then started singing with a smile of supreme contented bliss as she stared out to sea.

"What is she singing?" Bentley whispered to Marina.

"I think it's a *Yizkor*."

"A what?"

"A requiem."

"And that is…?"

"A remembrance mass… I imagine it's for Asher Worth."

Bentley nodded approvingly. Then he noticed the taut empty deck chair that had caught his attention on arrival seem to release its invisible guest. It was almost imperceptible, as thin as the air, but it disappeared on the wind and the ghost of Asher Worth had gone - now ready to meet his maker.

Hi there! MJ Colewood here. We hoped you enjoyed the book. If you did, we'd really appreciate it, if you could spare a few minutes to write a short review. Not only we will read what you have to say, but, more importantly, this will help us to spread the word about the Chester Bentley Mysteries, enabling others to take the plunge into the exciting adventures. Remember, if you're under 18 then you'll need your parents' consent. And if you've got any feedback or questions, we'd love to hear from you by dropping us a line over on our website. Hope to hear from you soon.

Seeing as you're still here, if you would like a <u>FREE</u> Chester Bentley mystery then you will find the first book in the series, an intriguing novella, which we refer to as book 'zero' as it is a prequel to the series, available for free download on our website at <u>www.mjcolewood.com</u>

FOLLOW THE <u>NEXT</u> CHESTER BENTLEY MYSTERY:

THE LAST TREASURE OF ANCIENT ENGLAND

It is 1066 and in the aftermath of the Battle of Hastings the mutilated corpse of King Harold has been looted. The disappearance of a particular item enrages Duke William, and only one of his knights knows its whereabouts. In his remaining years this knight has to make a decision: will he ever share his secret, or take the greatest enigma in English history to the grave?

Centuries later, when Chester Bentley arrives at his remote boarding school, he is unprepared for the mystery it conceals. The discovery of an age-old riddle lures him and his new friends into a quest to uncover the secrets safeguarded by the stately manor house. Hidden somewhere in the county of rural Devon is an extraordinary treasure and the school holds the puzzling key to its surprising location.

But something is lurking in the dark, shadowing them each time they venture out from their dormitory at night, and a ghostly legend puts fear into the bravest of pupils. In their last year at the school time is running out; so can they succeed where others have failed, and even died, in a chilling hunt to reveal the last treasure of ancient England?

Find out more at *www.mjcolewood.com*